TYRANTS
DESTROYED

Books by Vladimir Nabokov

Nabokov's Dozen, a collection of short stories

Nikolai Gogol, a critical biography

Pale Fire, a novel

Pnin, a novel

Poems and Problems

The Real Life of Sebastian Knight, a novel

A Russian Beauty and Other Stories

The Song of Igor's Campaign, Anon.,
  translated from Old Russian

Speak, Memory, a memoir

Strong Opinions, a collection of articles,
  letters, and interviews

Three Russian Poets, verse translation from the Russian

Transparent Things, a novel

Tyrants Destroyed and Other Stories

The Waltz Invention, a drama

VLADIMIR NABOKOV

TYRANTS DESTROYED
AND OTHER STORIES

McGraw-Hill Book Company
New York   •   Toronto

Book design by Marcy J. Katz.

Copyright © 1975 by Vladimir Nabokov.
All rights reserved.
Printed in the United States of America.
No part of this publication may
be reproduced, stored in a retrieval
system, or transmitted,
in any form or by any means,
electronic, mechanical, photocopying,
recording, or otherwise, without the prior written
permission of the publisher.

Library of Congress Cataloging in Publication Data

Nabokov, Vladimir Vladimirovich, 1899-
    Tyrants destroyed and other stories.

    "Of the thirteen stories in this collection the first
twelve have been translated from the Russian by Dmitri
Nabokov in collaboration with the author. The thir-
teenth story was written in English."
    CONTENTS: Tyrants destroyed.—A nursery tale.—Music.
—Lik.—Recruiting. [etc.]
    I. Title.
PZ3.N121Ty3   891.7'3'42   74-19209
ISBN 0-07-045739-5

"A Nursery Tale" and "The Admiralty Spire" originally
    appeared in *Playboy* Magazine.
"The Vane Sisters" was first published in *The Hudson
    Review*, Vol. XI, No. 4 (Winter 1958-1959).
"Bachmann" originally appeared in *Vogue* Magazine.
"Lik" and "Perfection" © 1974 by McGraw-Hill Inter-
    national, Inc. These stories originally appeared in
    The New Yorker.

123456789 BPBP 798765

To Véra

CONTENTS

Foreword

Of the thirteen stories in this collection the first twelve have been translated from the Russian by Dmitri Nabokov in collaboration with the author. They are representative of my carefree expatriate *tvorchestvo* (the dignified Russian word for "creative output") between 1924 and 1939, in Berlin, Paris, and Mentone. Bits of bibliography are given in the prefaces to them, and more information will be found in Andrew Field's *Nabokov: A Bibliography*, published by McGraw-Hill.

The thirteenth story was written in English in Ithaca, Upstate New York, at 802 East Seneca Street, a dismal grayish-white frame house, subjectively related to the more famous one at 342 Lawn Street, Ramsdale, New England.

Vladimir Nabokov
December 31, 1974
Montreux, Switzerland

TYRANTS
DESTROYED

Istreblenie Tiranov *was written in Mentone in spring or early summer 1938. It appeared in the* Russkiya Zapiski, *Paris, August 1938, and in my* Vesna v Fialte *collection of short stories, Chekhov House, New York, 1956. Hitler, Lenin, and Stalin dispute my tyrant's throne in this story— and meet again in* Bend Sinister, *1947, with a fifth toad. The destruction is thus complete.*

1

THE GROWTH of his power and fame was matched, in my imagination, by the degree of the punishment I would have liked to inflict on him. Thus, at first, I would have been content with an electoral defeat, a cooling of public enthusiasm. Later I already required his imprisonment; still later, his exile to some distant, flat island with a single palm tree, which, like a black asterisk, refers one to the bottom of an eternal hell made of solitude, disgrace, and helplessness. Now, at last, nothing but his death could satisfy me.

As in the graphs that visually demonstrate his ascension, indicating the number of his adherents by the gradual increase in size of a little figure that becomes biggish and then enormous, my hatred of him, its arms folded like those of his image, ominously swelled in the center of the space that was my soul, until it had nearly filled it, leaving me only a narrow rim of curved light (resembling more the corona of madness than the halo of martyrdom), though I foresee an utter eclipse still to come.

His first portraits, in the papers and shop windows and on the posters—which also kept growing in our abundantly irrigated, crying and bleeding country—looked rather blurred: this was when I still had doubts about the deadly outcome of my hatred. Something human, certain possibilities of his failing, his cracking, his falling ill, heaven knows what, came feebly shivering through some of his photographs in the random variety of not yet standardized poses and in a vacillating gaze which had not yet found its historical expression. Little by little, though, his countenance consolidated: his cheeks and cheekbones, in the official portrait photographs, became overlaid with a godly gloss, the olive oil of public affection, the varnish of a completed masterpiece; it became impossible to imagine that nose being blown, or that finger poking on the inside of that lip to extricate a food particle lodged behind a rotten incisor. Experimental variety was followed by a canonized uniformity that established the now familiar, stony, and lusterless, look of his neither intelligent nor cruel, but somehow unbearably eerie eyes. Established, too, was the solid fleshiness of his chin, the bronze of his jowls, and a feature that had already become the common property of all the cartoonists in the world and almost automatically brought off the trick of resemblance—a thick wrinkle across his whole forehead—the fatty sediment of thought, of course, rather than thought's scar. I am forced to believe that his face has been rubbed with all sorts of patent balsams, else I cannot comprehend its metallic good quality, for I once knew it when it was sickly, bloated, and ill-shaven, so that one heard the scrape of bristles against his dirty starch collar when he turned his head. And the glasses—what became of the glasses that he wore as a youth?

2

Not only have I never been fascinated by politics, but I have hardly ever read a single editorial or even a short report on a party congress. Sociological problems have never intrigued me, and to this day I cannot picture myself taking part in a conspiracy or simply sitting in a smoke-filled room among politically excited, tensely serious people, discussing methods of struggle in the light of recent developments. I don't give a hoot for the welfare of mankind, and not only do I not believe in any majority being automatically right, but tend to reexamine the question whether it is proper to strive for a state of affairs where literally everyone is half-fed and half-schooled. I further know that my fatherland, enslaved by him at the present time, is destined, in the distant future, to undergo many other upheavals, independent of any acts on *this* tyrant's part. Nevertheless, he must be killed.

3

When the gods used to assume earthly form and, clad in violet-tinted raiment, demurely but powerfully stepping with muscular feet in still dustless sandals, appeared to field laborers or mountain shepherds, their divinity was not in the least diminished for it; on the contrary, the charm of humanness enwafting them was a most eloquent reconfirmation of their celestial essence. But when a limited, coarse, little-educated man—at first glance a third-rate fanatic and in reality a pigheaded, brutal, and gloomy vulgarian full of morbid ambition—when such a man dresses up in godly garb, one feels like apologizing to the gods. It would be useless to try and convince me that actually he has nothing to do with it, that what elevated him to an iron-and-concrete throne, and now keeps him there, is the implacable evolution of dark, zoological, Zoorlandic ideas that have caught my fatherland's fancy. An idea selects only the helve; man is free to complete the ax—and use it.

Then again, let me repeat that I am no good at distinguishing what is good or bad for a state, and why it is that blood runs off it like water off a goose. Amid everybody and everything it is only one individual that interests me. That is my ailment, my obsession, and at the same time a thing that somehow belongs to me and that is entrusted to me alone for judgment. Since my early years—and I am no longer young—evil in people has struck me as particularly loathsome, unbearable to the point of suffocation and calling for immediate derision and destruction, whilst on the other hand I hardly noticed good in people, so much did it always seem to me the normal, indispensable condition, something granted and inalienable as, for example, the capacity to breathe is implied by the fact of being alive. With passing years I developed an extremely fine flair for evil, but my attitude toward good underwent a slight change, as I came to understand that its commonness, which had conditioned my indifference, was indeed so *uncommon* that I could not be sure at all of always finding it close to hand should the need arise. This is why I have led a hard, lonely life, always indigent, in shabby lodgings; yet I invariably had the obscure sensation of my real home being just around the corner, waiting for me, so that I could enter it as soon as I had finished with a thousand imaginary matters that cluttered my existence. Good God how I detested dull rectangular minds, how unfair I could be to a kindly person in whom I had happened to notice something comic, such as stinginess or respect for the well-to-do! And now I have before me not merely a weak solution of evil, such as can be obtained from any man, but a most highly concentrated, undiluted evil, in a huge vessel filled to the neck and sealed.

4

He transformed my wild-flowery country into a vast kitchen garden, where special care is lavished on turnips, cabbages, and beets; thus all the nation's passions were reduced to the passion for the fat vegetable in the good earth. A kitchen garden next to a factory with the inevitable accompaniment of a locomotive maneuvering somewhere in the background; the hopeless, drab sky of city outskirts, and everything the imagination associates with the scene: a fence, a rusted can among thistles, broken glass, excrements, a black, buzzing burst of flies under one's feet—this is the present-day image of my country. An image of the utmost dejection, but then dejection is in favor here, and a slogan *he* once tossed off (into the trash pit of stupidity)—"one half of our land must be cultivated, and the other asphalted"—is repeated by imbeciles as if it were a supreme expression of human happiness. There would be some excuse if he fed us the shoddy maxims he had once gleaned from reading sophists of the most banal kind, but he feeds us the chaff of those truths, and the manner of thinking required of us is based not simply on false wisdom, but on its rubble and stumblings. For me, however, the crux of the matter is not here either, for it stands to reason that even if the idea of which we are slaves were supremely inspired, exquisite, refreshingly moist, and sunny through and through, slavery would still be slavery inasmuch as the idea was inflicted on us. No, the point is that, as his power grew, I began to notice that the obligations of citizens, admonitions, restrictions, decrees, and all the other forms of pressure put on us were coming to resemble the man himself more and more closely, displaying an unmistakable relation to certain traits of his character and details of his past, so that on the basis of those admonitions and decrees one could reconstruct his personality like an octopus by its tentacles—that personality of his that I was one of the few to know well. In other words, everything around him began taking on his appearance. Legislation began to show a ludicrous likeness to his gait and gestures. Greengrocers began stocking a remarkable abundance of cucumbers, which he had so greedily consumed in his youth. The schools' curriculum now includes gypsy wrestling, which, in rare moments of cold playfulness, he used to practice on the floor with my brother twenty-five years ago. Newspaper articles and the novels of sycophantic writers have taken on that abruptness of style, that supposedly lapidary quality (basically senseless, for every minted phrase repeats in a different key one and the same official truism), that force of language *cum* weakness of thinking, and all those other stylistic affectations that are characteristic of him. I soon had the feeling that he, he as I remembered him, was penetrating everywhere, infecting with his presence the way of thinking and the everyday life of every person, so that his mediocrity, his tediousness, his gray habitude, were becoming the very life of my country. And finally the law he established—the implacable power of the majority, the incessant sacrifice to the idol of the majority—lost all sociological meaning, for *he* is the majority.

5

He was a comrade of my brother Gregory, who had a feverish, poetic passion for extreme forms of organized society (forms that had long been alarming the meek constitution we then had) in the final years of his short life: he drowned at twenty-three, bathing one summer evening in a wide, very wide river, so that when I now recall my brother the first thing that comes to my mind is a shiny spread of water, an islet overgrown with alder (that he never reached but toward which he always swims through the trembling haze of my memory), and a long, black cloud crossing another, opulently fluffed-up and orange-colored one, all that is left of a Saturday morning thunderstorm in the clear, turquoise Sunday's-eve sky, where a star will shine through in a moment, where there will never be any star. At that time I was much too engrossed in the history of painting and in my dissertation on its cave origins to frequent watchfully the group of young people that had inveigled my brother; for that matter, as I recall, there was no definite group, but simply several youths who had drifted together, different in many respects but, for the time being, loosely bound by a common attraction to rebellious adventure. The present, however, always exercises such a perverse influence on reminiscence that now I involuntarily single *him* out against that indistinct background, awarding him (neither the closest nor the most vociferous of Gregory's companions) the kind of somber, concentrated will deeply conscious of its sullen self, which in the end molds a giftless person into a triumphant monster.

I remember him waiting for my brother in the gloomy dining room of our humble provincial house; perching on the first chair he saw, he immediately began to read a rumpled newspaper extracted from a pocket of his black jacket, and his face, half-hidden by the armature of smoke-colored glasses, assumed a disgusted and weepy expression, as if he had hit upon some scurrilous stuff. I remember that his sloppily laced town boots were always dirty, as if he had just walked many miles along a cart road between unnoticed meadows. His cropped hair ended in a bristly wedge on his forehead (nothing foretold yet his present Caesar-like baldness). The nails of his large, humid hands were so closely bitten that it was painful to see the tight little cushions at the tips of his hideous fingers. He gave off a goatish smell. He was hard up, and indiscriminate as to sleeping quarters.

When my brother arrived (and in my recollection Gregory is always tardy, always comes in out of breath, as if

hastening terribly to live but arriving late all the same—
and thus it was that life finally left him behind), he greeted
Gregory without smiling, getting up abruptly and giving
his hand with an odd jerk, a kind of preliminary retraction
of the elbow; it seemed that if one did not snatch his hand
in time it would bounce back, with a springy click, into its
detachable cuff. If some member of our family entered, he
limited himself to a surly nod; per contra, he would de-
monstratively shake hands with the cook, who, taken by
surprise and not having time to wipe her palm before the
clasp, wiped it afterwards, in a retake of the scene, as it
were. My mother died not long before his first visits, while
my father's attitude toward him was as absentminded as it
was toward everyone and everything—toward us, toward
life's adversities, toward the presence of grubby dogs to
whom Gregory offered shelter, and even, it seems, toward
his patients. On the other hand, two elderly aunts of mine
were openly wary of the "eccentric" (if anyone ever was
the opposite of eccentric it was he) as, for that matter,
they were of Gregory's other pals.

Now, twenty-five years later, I often have occasion to
hear his voice, his bestial roar, diffused by the thunders of
radio; back then, however, I recall he always spoke softly,
even with a certain huskiness, a certain susurrous lisp. Only
that famous vile bit of breathlessness of his, at the end of a
sentence, was already there, yes, already there. When he
stood, head and arms lowered, before my brother, who was
greeting him with affectionate exclamations, still trying to
catch at least an elbow of his, or his bony shoulder, he
seemed curiously short-legged, owing, probably, to the
length of his jacket, which came down to mid-hip; and one
could not determine whether the mournfulness of his pos-

ture was caused by glum shyness or by a straining of the faculties before uttering some tragic message. Later it seemed to me that he had at last uttered it and done with it, when, on that dreadful summer evening, he came from the river carrying what looked like a heap of clothes but was only Gregory's shirt and canvas pants; now, however, I think that the message he seemed to be always pregnant with was not that one after all, but the muffled news of his own monstrous future.

Sometimes, through a half-open door, I could hear his abnormally halting speech in a talk with my brother; or he would be sitting at the tea table, breaking a pretzel, his night-bird eyes turned away from the light of the kerosene lamp. He had a strange and unpleasant way of rinsing his mouth with his milk before he swallowed it, and when he bit into the pretzel he cautiously twisted his mouth; his teeth were bad, and to deceive the fiery pain of a bared nerve by a brief whiff of coolness, he would repeatedly suck in the air, with a sidewise whistle. Once, I remember, my father soaked a bit of cottonwool for him with some brown drops containing opium and, chuckling aimlessly, recommended that he see a dentist. "The whole is stronger than its parts," he answered with awkward gruffness, "*ergo* I will vanquish my tooth." I am no longer certain, though, whether I heard those wooden words personally, or whether they were subsequently repeated to me as a pronouncement by the "eccentric"; only, as I have already said, he was nothing of the sort, for how can an animal faith in one's blear guiding star be regarded as something peculiar and rare? But, believe it or not, he impressed people with his mediocrity as others do with their talent.

6

Sometimes his innate mournfulness was broken by spasms of nasty, jagged joviality, and then I would hear his laughter, as jarring and unexpected as the yowl of a cat, to whose velvet silence you grow so accustomed that its nocturnal voice seems a demented, demonic thing. Shrieking thus, he would be drawn by his companions into games and tussles; it turned out then that he had the arms of a weakling, but legs strong as steel. On one occasion a particularly prankish boy put a toad in his pocket, whereupon he, being afraid to go after it with his fingers, started tearing off the weighted jacket and in that state, his face darkly flushed, disheveled, with nothing but a dicky over his torn undershirt, he fell prey to a heartless hunchbacked girl, whose massive braid and ink-blue eyes were so attractive to many that she was willingly forgiven a resemblance to a black chess knight.

I know about his amorous tendencies and system of courtship from that very girl, now, unfortunately, deceased, like the majority of those who knew him well in his youth (as if death were an ally of his, removing from his path dangerous witnesses to his past). To this vivacious hunchback he would write either in a didactic tone, with excursions—of a popular-educational type—into history (which he knew from political pamphlets), or else complain in obscure and soggy terms about another woman (also with a physical defect of some kind, I believe), who remained unknown to me, and with whom at one time he had shared bed and board in the most dismal part of the city. Today I would give a lot to search out and interrogate that anonymous person, but she, too, no doubt, is safely dead. A curious feature of his missives was their noisome wordiness: he hinted at the machinations of mysterious enemies; polemicized at length with some poetaster, whose verselets he had read in a calendar—oh, if it were possible to resurrect those precious exercise-book pages, filled with his minuscule, myopic handwriting! Alas, I do not recall a single phrase from them (at the time I was not very interested, even if I did listen and chuckle), and only very indistinctly do I see, in the depths of memory, the bow on that braid, the thin clavicle, and the quick, dusky hand in the garnet bracelet crumpling his letters; and I also catch the cooing note of perfidious feminine laughter.

7

The difference between dreaming of a reordered world and dreaming of reordering it oneself as one sees fit is a profound and fatal one; yet none of his friends, including my brother, apparently made any distinction between their abstract rebellion and *his* merciless lust for power. A month after my brother's death he vanished, transferring his activity to the northern provinces (my brother's group withered and fell apart and, as far as I know, none of its other participants went into politics), and soon there were rumors that the work being done there, both in its aims and methods, had grown diametrically opposed to all that had been said, thought, and hoped in that initial young circle. When I recall his aspect in those days, I find it amazing that no one noticed the long, angular shadow of treason that he dragged behind him wherever he went, tucking its fringe under the furniture when he sat down, and letting it interfere strangely with the banister's own shadow on the wall of the staircase, down which he was seen to the door by the light of a portable kerosene lamp. Or is it our dark present time that was cast forward there?

I do not know if they liked him, but in any case my brother and the others mistook his moroseness for the intensity of spiritual force. The cruelty of his ideas seemed a natural consequence of enigmatic calamities he had suffered; and his whole unprepossessive shell presupposed, as it were, a clean, bright kernel. I may as well confess that I myself once had the fleeting impression that he was capable of mercy; only subsequently did I determine its true shade. Those who are fond of cheap paradoxes took note long ago of the sentimentality of executioners; and indeed, the sidewalk in front of butcher shops is always dampish.

8

The first days after the tragedy he kept turning up, and several times spent the night in our place. That death did not evoke any visible signs of grief in him. He behaved as always, which did not shock us in the least, since his usual state was already mournful: and as usual he would sit in some corner, reading something uninteresting and behaving, in short, as, in a house where a great misfortune has occurred, people do who are neither close intimates nor complete strangers. Now, moreover, his constant presence and sullen silence could pass for grim commiseration—the commiseration, you see, of a strong reticent man, inconspicuous but ever-present—a very pillar of sympathy—about whom you later learn that he himself was seriously ill at the time he spent those sleepless nights on a chair among tear-blinded members of the household. In his case, however, this was all a dreadful misconception: if he did feel drawn to our house at the time, it was solely because nowhere did he breathe so naturally as in the sphere of gloom and despair, when uncleared dishes litter the table and nonsmokers ask for cigarettes.

I vividly remember setting out with him to perform one of the minor formalities, one of the excruciatingly dim bits of business with which death (having, as it always has, an element of red tape about it) tries to entangle survivors for as long as possible. Probably someone said to me, "There, *he* will go with you," and he came, discreetly clearing his throat. It was on that occasion (we were walking along a houseless street, fluffy with dust, past fences and piles of lumber) that I did something the memory of which traverses me from top to toe like an electrical jolt of insufferable shame: driven by God knows what feeling—perhaps not so much by gratitude as by condolence for another's condolence—in a surge of nervousness and ill-timed emotion, I clasped and squeezed his hand (which caused us both to stumble slightly). It all lasted an instant, and yet, if I had then embraced him and pressed my lips to his horrible golden bristles, I could not have felt any greater torment now. Now, after twenty-five years, I wonder: the two of us were walking alone through a deserted neighborhood, and in my pocket I had Gregory's loaded revolver, which, for some reason or other, I kept meaning to hide; I could perfectly well have dispatched him with a shot at point-blank range, and then there would have been nothing of what there is today—no rain-drenched holidays, no gigantic festivities with millions of my fellow citizens marching by with shovels, hoes, and rakes on their slavish shoulders; no loudspeakers, deafeningly multiplying the same inescapable voice; no secret mourning in every other family, no assortment of tortures, no torpor of the mind, no colossal portraits—nothing. Oh if it were possible to claw into the past, drag a missed opportunity by its hair back into the present, resurrect that dusty street, the vacant lots, the weight in my hip pocket, the youth walking at my side!

9

I am dull and fat, like Prince Hamlet. What can I do? Between me, a humble teacher of drawing in a provincial high school, and him, sitting behind a multitude of steel and oaken doors in an unknown chamber of the capital's main jail, transformed for him into a castle (for this tyrant calls himself "prisoner of the will of the people that elected him") there is an unimaginable distance. Someone was telling me, after having locked himself in the basement with me, about an old widow, a distant relative of his, who succeeded in growing an eighty-pound turnip, thus meriting an audience with the exalted one. She was conducted through one marble corridor after another, and an endless succession of doors was unlocked in front of her and locked behind her, until she found herself in a white, starkly lit hall, whose entire furnishings consisted of two gilt chairs. Here she was told to stand and wait. In due time she heard numerous footfalls from behind the door, and, with respectful bows, deferring to each other, half a dozen of his bodyguards came in. With frightened eyes she searched for *him* among them; their eyes were directed not at her but somewhere beyond her head; then, turning, she saw that behind her, through another, unnoticed door, he himself had noiselessly entered and, having stopped and placed a hand on the back of one of the two chairs, was scrutinizing the guest of the State with a habitual air of encouragement. Then he seated himself and suggested that she describe in her own words her glorious achievement (here an attendant brought in and placed on the second chair a clay replica of her vegetable), and, for ten unforgettable minutes, she narrated how she had planted the turnip; how she had tugged and tugged without being able to get it out of the ground, even though she thought she saw her deceased husband tugging with her; how she had had to call first her son, then her nephew and even a couple of firemen who were resting in the hayloft; and how, finally, backing in tandem arrangement, they had extracted the monster. Evidently he was overwhelmed by her vivid narrative; "Now that's genuine poetry," he said, addressing his retinue. "Here's somebody the poet fellows ought to learn from."

And, crossly ordering that the likeness be cast in bronze, he left. I, however, do not grow turnips, so I cannot find a way to him; and, even if I did, how would I carry my treasured weapon to his lair?

On occasion he appears before the people, and, even though no one is allowed near him, and everyone has to hold up the heavy staff of an issued banner so that hands are kept busy, and everyone is watched by a guard of incalculable proportions (to say nothing of the secret agents and the secret agents watching the secret agents), someone very adroit and resolute might have the good fortune to find a loophole, one transparent instant, some tiny chink of fate through which to rush forward. I mentally considered, one by one, all kinds of destructive means, from the classic dagger to plebeian dynamite, but it was all in vain, and it is with good reason that I frequently dream I am repeatedly squeezing the trigger of a weapon that is disintegrating in my hand, whilst the bullets trickle out of the barrel, or bounce like harmless peas off the chest of my grinning foe while he begins unhurriedly to crush my rib cage.

10

Yesterday I invited several people, unacquainted among themselves but united by one and the same sacred task, which had so transfigured them that one could notice among them an inexpressible resemblance, such as occurs, for instance, among elderly Freemasons. They were people

of various professions—a tailor, a masseur, a physician, a
barber, a baker—but all exhibited the same dignified de-
portment, the same economy of gestures. And no wonder!
One made his clothes, and that meant measuring his lean,
yet broad-hipped body, with its odd, womanish pelvis and
round back, and respectfully reaching into his armpits, and,
together with him, looking into a mirror garlanded with
gilt ivy; the second and third had penetrated even further:
they had seen him naked, had kneaded his muscles and listened to his heart, by whose beat, it is said, our clocks will
soon be set, so that his pulse, in the most literal sense, will
become a basic unit of time; the fourth shaved him, with
crepitating strokes, down on the cheeks and on the neck,
using a blade that to me is enticingly sharp-looking; the
fifth, and last, baked his bread, putting, the idiot, through
sheer force of habit raisins instead of arsenic into his favorite loaf. I wanted to palpate these people, so as to par-
take at least in that way of their mysterious rites, of their
diabolical manipulations; it seemed to me that their hands
were imbued with his smell, that through those people he,
too, was present. It was all very nice, very prim at that
party. We talked about things that did not concern him,
and I knew that if I mentioned his name there would flash
in the eyes of each of them the same sacerdotal alarm. And
when I suddenly found myself wearing a suit cut by my
neighbor on the right, and eating my vis-à-vis' pastry,
which I washed down with a special kind of mineral water
prescribed by my neighbor on the left, I was overcome by
a dreadful, dream-significant feeling, which immediately
awakened me—in my poor-man's room, with a poor-man's
moon in the curtainless window.

I am grateful to the night for even such a dream: of late

Tyrants Destroyed

I have been racked by insomnia. It is as if his agents were accustoming me beforehand to the most popular of the tortures inflicted on present-day criminals. I write "present-day" because, since he came to power, there has appeared a completely new breed, as it were, of political criminals (the other, penal, kind actually no longer exists, as the pettiest theft swells into embezzlement which, in turn, is considered an attempt to undermine the regime), exquisitely frail creatures, with a most diaphanous skin and protruding eyes emitting bright rays. This is a rare and highly valued breed, like a young okapi or the smallest species of lemur; they are hunted passionately, self-obliviously, and every captured specimen is hailed by public applause, even though the hunt actually involves no particular difficulty or danger, for they are quite tame, those strange, transparent beasts.

Timorous rumor has it that he himself is not loath to pay an occasional visit to the torture chamber, but there is probably no truth in this: the postmaster general does not distribute the mail himself, nor is the secretary of the navy necessarily a crack swimmer. I am in general repelled by the homey, gossipy tone with which meek ill-wishers speak of him, getting sidetracked into a special kind of primitive joke, as, in olden times, the common people would make up stories about the devil, dressing up their superstitious fear in buffoonish humor. Vulgar, hastily adapted anecdotes (dating back, say, to Celtic prototypes), or secret information "from a usually reliable source" (as to who, for instance, is in favor and who is not) always smack of the servants' quarters. There are even worse examples, though: when my friend N., whose parents were executed only three years ago (to say nothing of the disgraceful persecution N. himself underwent), remarks, upon his return from an official festivity where he has heard and seen him, "You know, though, in spite of everything, there is a certain strength about that man," I feel like punching N. in the mug.

11

In the published letters of his "Sunset Years" a universally acclaimed foreign writer mentions that everything now leaves him cold, disenchanted, indifferent, everything with one exception: the vital, romantic thrill that he experiences to this day at the thought of how squalid his youthful years were compared with the sumptuous fulfillment of his later life, and of the snowy gleam of its summit, which he has now reached. That initial insignificance, that penumbra of poetry and pain, in which the young artist is on a par with a million such insignificant fellow beings, now lures him and fills him with excitement and gratitude—to his destiny, to his craft—and to his own creative will. Visits to places, where he had once lived in want, and reunions with his coevals, elderly men of no note whatsoever, hold for him such a complex wealth of enchantment that the detailed study of these sensations will last him for his soul's future leisure in the hereafter.

Thus, when I try to imagine what our lugubrious ruler feels upon contact with *his* past, I clearly understand, first,

that the real human being is a poet and, second, that he, our
ruler, is the incarnate negation of a poet. And yet the foreign papers, especially those whose names have vesperal
connotations and which know how easily "tales" can be
transformed into "sales," are fond of stressing the legendary
quality of his destiny, guiding its crowd of readers into the
enormous black house where he was born, and where supposedly to this day live similar paupers, endlessly hanging
out the wash (paupers do a great deal of washing); and
they also print a photo, obtained God knows how, of his
progenitress (father unknown), a thickset broad-nosed
woman with a fringe who worked in an alehouse at the
city gate. So few eyewitnesses of his boyhood and youth
remain, and those who are still around respond with such
circumspection (alas, no one has questioned *me*) that a
journalist needs a great gift for invention to portray today's
ruler excelling at warlike games as a boy or, as a youth,
reading books till cockcrow. His demagogic luck is con-
strued to be the elemental force of destiny, and, naturally,
a great deal of attention is devoted to that overcast winter
day when, upon his election to parliament, he and his gang
arrested the parliament (after which the army, bleating
meekly, went over at once to his side).

Not much of a myth, but still a myth (in this nuance the
journalist was not mistaken), a myth that is a closed circle
and a discrete whole, ready to begin living its own, insular
life, and it is *already* impossible to replace it with the real
truth, even though its hero is still alive: impossible, since
he, the only one who could know the truth, is useless as a
witness, and this not because he is prejudiced or dishonest,
but because, like a runaway slave, he "doesn't remember"!

Oh, he remembers his old enemies, of course, and two or three books he has read, and how the man thrashed him for falling off a woodpile and crushing to death a couple of chicks: that is, a certain crude mechanism of memory does function in him, but, if the gods were to propose that he synthesize himself out of his memories, with the condition that the synthesized image be rewarded with immortality, the result would be a dim embryo, an infant born prematurely, a blind and deaf dwarf, in no sense capable of immortality.

Should he visit the house where he lived when he was poor, no thrill would ripple his skin—not even a thrill of malevolent vanity. But I did visit his former abode! Not the multiplex edifice where he is supposed to have been born, and where there is now a museum dedicated to him (old posters, a flag grimy with gutter mud, in the place of honor, under a bell jar, a button: all that it was possible to preserve of his niggardly youth), but those vile furnished rooms where he spent several months during the period he and my brother were close. The former proprietor had long since died, roomers had never been registered, so that no trace was left of his erstwhile sojourn. And the thought that I alone in the world (for he has forgotten those lodgings of his—there have been so many) *knew* about this filled me with a special satisfaction, as if, by touching that dead furniture and looking at the neighboring roof through the window, I felt my hand closing on the key to his life.

12

I have just had yet another visitor: a very seedy old man, who was evidently in a state of extreme agitation: his tight-skinned, glossy-backed hands were trembling, a stale senile tear dampened the pink lining of his eyelids, and a pallid sequence of involuntary expressions, from a foolish smile to a crooked crease of pain, passed across his face. With the pen I lent him he traced on a scrap of paper the digits of a crucial year, day, and month: the date—nearly half-a-century past—of the ruler's birth. He rested his gaze on me, pen raised, as if not daring to continue, or simply using a semblance of hesitation to emphasize the little trick he was about to play. I answered with a nod of encouragement and impatience, whereupon he wrote another date, preceding the first by nine months, underlined it twice, parted his lips as if for a burst of triumphant laughter, but, instead, suddenly covered his face with his hands. "Come on, get to the point," I said, giving this indifferent actor's shoulder a shake. Quickly regaining his composure, he rummaged in his pocket and handed me a thick, stiff photograph, which, over the years, had acquired an opaque milky tint. It showed a husky young man in a soldier's uniform; his peaked cap lay on a chair, on whose back, with wooden ease, he rested his hand, while behind him you could make out the ballustrade and the urn of a conventional backdrop. With the help of two or three connective glances I ascertained that between my guest's features and the shadowless, flat face of the soldier (adorned with a thin mustache, and topped by a brush cut, which made the forehead look smaller) there was little resemblance, but that nevertheless the soldier and he were the same person. In the snapshot he was about twenty, the snapshot itself was some fifty years old, and it was easy to fill this interval with the trite account of one of those third-rate lives, the imprint of which one reads (with an agonizing sense of superiority, sometimes unjustified) on the faces of old ragmen, public-garden attendants, and embittered invalids in the uniforms of old wars. I was about to pump him as to how it felt to live with such a secret, how he could carry the weight of that monstrous paternity, and incessantly see and hear his offspring's public presence—but then I noticed that the mazy and issueless design of the wallpaper was showing through his body; I stretched out my hand to detain my guest, but the dodderer dissolved, shivering from the chill of vanishment.

And yet he exists, this father (or existed until quite recently), and if only fate did not bestow on him a salutary ignorance as to the identity of his momentary bedmate, God knows what torment is at large among us, not daring to speak out, and perhaps made even more acute by the fact that the hapless fellow is not fully certain of his pater-nity, for the wench was a loose one, and in consequence there might be several like him in the world, indefatigably calculating dates, blundering in the hell of too many fig-ures and too meager memories, ignobly dreaming of ex-tracting profit from the shadows of the past, fearing instant punishment (for some error, or blasphemy, for the too odious truth), feeling rather proud in their heart of hearts (after all he is the Ruler!), losing their mind between supputation and supposition—horrible, horrible!

13

Time passes, and meanwhile I get bogged down in wild, oppressive fancies. In fact, it astonishes me, for I know of a good number of resolute and even daring actions that I have to my credit, nor am I in the least afraid of the perilous consequences that an assassination attempt would have for me; on the contrary, while I have no clear idea at all of how the act itself will occur, I can make out distinctly the tussle that will immediately follow—the human tornado seizing me, the puppetlike jerkiness of my motions amid avid hands, the crack of clothes being ripped, the blinding red of the blows, and finally (should I emerge from this tussle alive) the iron grip of jailers, imprisonment, a swift trial, the torture chamber, the scaffold, all this to the thundering accompaniment of my mighty happiness. I do not expect that my fellow citizens will immediately perceive their own liberation; I can even allow that the regime might get harsher out of sheer inertia. There is nothing about me of the civic hero who dies for his people. I die only for myself, for the sake of my own world of good and truth—the good and the true, which are now distorted and violated within me and outside me, and if they are as precious to someone else as they are to me, all the better; if not, if my fatherland needs men of a different stamp than I, I willingly accept my uselessness, but will still perform my task.

My life is too much engrossed and submerged by my hatred to be in the least pleasant, and I do not fear the black nausea and agony of death, especially since I anticipate a degree of bliss, a level of supernatural being undreamt of either by barbarians or by modern followers of old religions. Thus, my mind is lucid and my hand free— and yet I don't know, I don't know how to go about killing him.

I sometimes think that perhaps it is so because murder, the intent to kill, is after all unsufferably trite, and the imagination, reviewing methods of homicide and types of weapons, performs a degrading task, the sham of which is the more keenly felt, the more righteous the force that impels one. Or else, maybe I could not kill him out of squeamishness, as some people, while they feel a fierce aversion to anything that crawls, are unable so much as to crush a garden worm underfoot because for them it would be like stamping on the dust-begrimed extremities of their own innards. But whatever explanations I conjure up for my irresoluteness, it would be foolish to hide from myself the fact that I must destroy him. O Hamlet, O moony oaf!

14

He has just given a speech at the groundbreaking ceremony for a new, multistoried greenhouse, and, while he was at it, he touched on the equality of men and the equality of wheat ears in the field, using Latin or dog-Latin, for the sake of poetry, *arista*, *aristifer*, and even "aristize" (meaning "to ear")—I do not know what corny schoolman counseled him to adopt this questionable method, but, in recompense, I now understand why, of late, magazine verse contains such archaisms as:

> *How sapient the veterinarian*
> *Who physics the lactific kine.*

For two hours the enormous voice thundered throughout our city, erupting with varying degrees of force from this or that window, so that, if you walk along a street (which, by the way, is deemed a dangerous discourtesy: sit and listen), you have the impression that he accompanies you, crashing down from the rooftops, squirming on all fours between your legs, and sweeping up again to peck at your head, cackling, cawing, and quacking in a caricature of human speech, and you have no place to hide from the Voice, and the same thing is going on in every city and village of my successfully stunned country. Apparently no one except me has noticed an interesting feature of his frenzied oratory, namely the pause he makes after a particularly effective sentence, rather like a drunk who stands in the middle of the street, in the independent but unsatisfied solitude characteristic of drunks, and while declaiming fragments of an abusive monologue, most emphatic in its wrath, passion, and conviction, but obscure as to meaning and aim, stops frequently to collect his strength, ponder the next passage, let what he has said sink in; then, having waited out the pause, he repeats verbatim what he has just disgorged, but in a tone of voice suggesting that he has thought of a new argument, another absolutely new and irrefutable idea.

When the Ruler at last ran dry, and the faceless, cheek-less trumpets played our agrarian anthem, I not only did not feel relieved, but, on the contrary, had a sense of anguish and loss: while he was speaking I could at least keep watch over him, could know where he was and what he was doing; now he has again dissolved into the air, which I breathe but which has no tangible point of focus.

I can understand the smooth-haired women of our mountain tribes when, abandoned by a lover, every morning, with a persistent pressure of their brown fingers on the turquoise head of a pin, they prick the navel of a clay figurine representing the fugitive. Many times, of late, I have summoned all the force of my mind to imagine at a given moment the flow of his cares and thoughts, in order to duplicate the rhythm of his existence, making it yield and come crashing down, like a suspension bridge whose own oscillations have coincided with the cadenced step of a detachment of soldiers crossing it. The soldiers will also perish—so shall I, losing my reason the instant that I catch the rhythm, while he falls dead in his distant castle; however, no matter what the method of tyrannicide, I would not survive. When I wake up in the morning, at half-past-eight or so, I strain to conjure up his awakening: he gets up neither early nor late, at an average hour, just as he calls himself—even officially, I think—an "average man." At nine both he and I breakfast frugally on a glass of milk and a bun, and, if on a given day I am not busy at the school, I continue my pursuit of his thoughts. He reads through several newspapers, and I read them with him, searching for something that might catch his attention, even though I know he was aware the evening before of the general content of my morning paper, of its leading articles, its summaries and national news, so that this perusal

can give him no particular cause for administrative medita-
tion. After which his assistants come with reports and
queries. Together with him, I learn how rail communica-
tions are feeling today, how heavy industry is sweating
along, and how many centners per hectare the winter
wheat crop yielded this year. After looking through several
petitions for clemency and tracing on them his invariable
refusal—a penciled "X"—the symbol of his heart's illiteracy
—he takes his usual walk before lunch: as in the case of
many not overbright people devoid of imagination, walking
is his favorite exercise; he walks in his walled garden, formerly a large prison yard. I am also familiar with the menu
of his unpretentious lunch, after which I share my siesta
with him and ponder plans for making his power flourish
further, or new measures for suppressing sedition. In the
afternoon we inspect a new building, a fortress, a forum,
and other forms of governmental prosperity, and I approve
with him an inventor's new kind of ventilator. I skip dinner,
usually a gala affair with various functionaries in atten-
dance, but, on the other hand, by nightfall my thoughts
have redoubled their force and I issue orders to newspaper
editors, listen to accounts of evening meetings and, alone in
my darkening room, whisper, gesticulate, and ever more
insanely hope that at least one of my thoughts may fall in
step with a thought of his—and then, I know, the bridge
will snap, like a violin string. But the ill luck familiar to
overly eager gamblers haunts me, the right card never
comes, even though I must have achieved a certain secret
liaison with him, for around eleven o'clock, when he goes
to bed, my entire being senses a collapse, a void, a weak-
ening, and a melancholy relief. Presently he sleeps, he
sleeps, and, since, on his convict's cot, not a single praedor-

mitory thought troubles him, I too am left at liberty, and only occasionally, without the least hope of success, try to compose his dreams, combining fragments of his past with impressions of the present; probably, though, he does not dream and I work in vain, and never, never, will the night be rent by a royal death rattle, leading history to comment: "The dictator died in his sleep."

15

How can I get rid of him? I cannot stand it any longer. Everything is full of him, everything I love has been besmirched, everything has become his likeness, his mirror image, and, in the features of passersby and in the eyes of my wretched schoolchildren, his countenance shows ever clearer and more hopelessly. Not only the posters that I am obliged to have them copy in color do nothing but interpret the pattern of his personality, but even the simple white cube I give the younger classes to draw seems to me his portrait—perhaps his best portrait. O cubic monster, how can I eradicate you?

16

And suddenly I realized I had a way! It was on a frosty, motionless morning, with a pale pink sky and lumps of ice lodged in the drainpipes' jaws; there was a doomful stillness everywhere: in an hour the town would awake, and how it would awake! That day his fiftieth birthday was to be celebrated, and already people, looking against the snow like black quarter notes, were creeping out into the streets, so as to gather on schedule at the points where they would be marshaled into different marching groups determined by their trades. At the risk of losing my meager pay, I was not making ready to join any festive procession; I had something else, a little more important, on my mind. Standing by the window, I could hear the first distant fanfares and the radio barker's inducements at the crossroads, and I found comfort in the thought that I, and I alone, could interrupt all this. Yes, the solution had been found: the assassination of the tyrant now turned out to be something so simple and quick that I could accomplish it without leaving my room. The only weapons available for the purpose were either an old but very well preserved revolver, or a hook over the window that must have served at one time to support a drapery rod. This last was even better, as I had my doubts about the performance of the twenty-five-year-old cartridge.

By killing myself I would kill him, as he was totally inside me, fattened on the intensity of my hatred. Along with him I would kill the world he had created, all the stupidity, cowardice, and cruelty of that world, which, together with him, had grown huge within me, ousting, to the last sun-bathed landscape, to the last memory of childhood, all the treasures I had collected. Conscious now of my power, I reveled in it, unhurriedly preparing for self-destruction, going through my belongings, correcting this chronicle of mine. And then, abruptly, the incredible intensification of all the senses that had overwhelmed me underwent a strange, almost alchemic metamorphosis. The festivities were spreading outside my window, the sun transformed the blue snowdrifts into sparkling down, and one could see playing over distant roofs, a new kind of fireworks (invented recently by a peasant genius) whose colors blazed even in broad daylight. The general jubilation; the Ruler's gem-bright likeness flashing pyrotechnically in the heavens; the gay hues of the procession winding across the river's snowy cover; the delightful pasteboard symbols of the fatherland's welfare; the slogans, designed with variety and elegance, that bobbed above the marchers' shoulders; the jaunty primitive music; the orgy of banners; the contented faces of the young yokels and the national costumes of the hefty wenches—all of it caused a crimson wave of tenderness to surge within me, and I understood my sin against our great and merciful Master. Is it not he who manured our fields, who directed the poor to be shod, he whom we must thank for every second of our civic being? Tears of repentance, hot, good tears, gushed from my eyes onto the window sill when I thought how I had been repudiating the kindness of the Master, how blindly I had reneged the beauty of what he had created, the social order, the way of life, the splendid walnut-finished new fences, and how I plotted to lay hands on myself, daring, thus, to endanger the life of one of his subjects! The festivities, as I have said, were spreading; I stood at the window, my whole being drenched with tears and convulsed with laughter, listening to the verses of our foremost poet, declaimed on the radio by an actor's juicy voice, replete with baritone modulations:

> Now then, citizens,
> You remember how long
> Our land wilted without a Father?
> Thus, without hops, no matter how strong
> One's thirst, it is rather
> Difficult, isn't it,
> To make both the beer and the drinking song!
> Just imagine, we lacked potatoes,
> No turnips, no beets could we get:
> Thus the poem, now blooming, wasted
> In the bulbs of the alphabet!
> A well-trodden road we had taken,
> Bitter toadstools we ate,
> Until by great thumps was shaken
> History's gate!
> Until in his trim white tunic
> Which upon us its radiance cast,
> With his wonderful smile the Ruler
> Came before his subjects at last!

Yes, "radiance," yes, "toadstools," yes, "wonderful," that's right. I, a little man, I, the blind beggar who today has gained his sight, fall on my knees and repent before you. Execute me—no, even better, pardon me, for the block is your pardon, and your pardon the block, illuminating with an aching, benignant light the whole of my iniquity. You are our pride, our glory, our banner! O magnificent, gentle giant, who intently and lovingly watches

over us, I swear to serve you from this day on, I swear to
be like all your other nurslings, I swear to be yours indi-
visibly, and so forth, and so forth, and so forth.

17

Laughter, actually, saved me. Having experienced all the
degrees of hatred and despair, I achieved those heights from
which one obtains a bird's-eye view of the ludicrous. A
roar of hearty mirth cured me, as it did, in a children's
storybook, the gentleman "in whose throat an abscess burst
at the sight of a poodle's hilarious tricks." Rereading my
chronicle, I see that, in my efforts to make him terrifying,
I have only made him ridiculous, thereby destroying him—
an old, proven method. Modest as I am in evaluating my
muddled composition, something nevertheless tells me that
it is not the work of an ordinary pen. Far from having
literary aspirations, and yet full of words forged over the
years in my enraged silence, I have made my point with
sincerity and fullness of feeling where another would have
made it with artistry and inventiveness. This is an incanta-
tion, an exorcism, so that henceforth any man can exorcise
bondage. I believe in miracles. I believe that in some way,
unknown to me, this chronicle will reach other men, neither tomorrow nor the next day, but at a distant time when
the world has a day or so of leisure for archeological dig-
gings, on the eve of new annoyances, no less amusing than
the present ones. And, who knows—I may be right not to

rule out the thought that my chance labor may prove immortal, and may accompany the ages, now persecuted, now exalted, often dangerous, and always useful. While I, a "boneless shadow," *un fantôme sans os*, will be content if the fruit of my forgotten insomnious nights serves for a long time as a kind of secret remedy against future tyrants, tigroid monsters, half-witted torturers of man.

A NURSERY TALE

A Nursery Tale (Skazka *in Russian*) *was written in Berlin, in late May or early June 1926, and serialized in the émigré daily Rul'* (Berlin), *in the issues of June 27 and 29 of that year. It was reprinted in my* Vozvrashchenie Chorba *collection, Slovo publishers, Berlin, 1930.*

A rather artificial affair, composed a little hastily, with more concern for the tricky plot than for imagery and good taste, it required some revamping here and there in the English version. Young Erwin's harem, however, has remained intact. I had not reread my Skazka since 1930 and, when working now at its translation, was eerily startled to meet a somewhat decrepit but unmistakable Humbert escorting his nymphet in the story I wrote almost half-a-century ago.

1

FANTASY, THE flutter, the rapture of fantasy! Erwin knew these things well. In a tram, he would always sit on the right-hand side, so as to be nearer the sidewalk. Twice daily, from the tram he took to the office and back, Erwin looked out of the window and collected his harem. Happy, happy Erwin, to dwell in such a convenient, such a fairy-tale German town!

He covered one sidewalk in the morning, on his way to work, and the other in the late afternoon, on his way home. First one, then the other was bathed in voluptuous sunlight, for the sun also went and returned. We should bear in mind that Erwin was so morbidly shy that only once in his life, taunted by rascally comrades, he had accosted a woman, and she had said quietly: "You ought to be ashamed of yourself. Leave me alone." Thereafter, he had avoided conversation with strange young ladies. In compensation, separated from the street by a windowpane, clutching to his ribs a black briefcase, wearing scuffed trousers with a pin-stripe, and stretching one leg under the opposite seat (if unoccupied), Erwin looked boldly and freely at passing girls, and then would suddenly bite his nether lip: this signified the capture of a new concubine; whereupon he would set her aside, as it were, and his swift gaze, jumping like a compass needle, was already seeking out the next one. Those beauties were far from him, and therefore the sweetness of free choice could not be affected by sullen timidity. If however a girl happened to sit down across from him, and a certain twinge told him that she was pretty, he would retract his leg from under her seat with all the signs of a gruffness quite uncharacteristic of his young age—and could not bring himself to take stock of her: the bones of his forehead—right here, over the eyebrows—ached from shyness, as if an iron helmet were restricting his temples and preventing him from raising his eyes; and what a relief it was when she got up and went toward the exit. Then, feigning casual abstraction, he looked—shameless Erwin did look—following her receding back, swallowing whole her adorable nape and silk-hosed calves, and thus, after all, would he add her to his fabulous harem! The leg would again be stretched, again the bright sidewalk would flow past the window, and again, his thin pale nose with a noticeable depression at the tip directed streetward, Erwin would accumulate his slave girls. And this is fantasy, the flutter, the rapture of fantasy!

2

One Saturday, on a frivolous evening in May, Erwin was sitting at a sidewalk table. He watched the tripping throng of the avenue, now and then biting his lip with a quick incisor. The entire sky was tinged with pink and the street-lamps and shop-sign bulbs glowed with a kind of unearthly light in the gathering dusk. The first lilacs were being hawked by an anemic but pretty young girl. Rather fittingly the café phonograph was singing the Flower Aria from *Faust*.

A tall middle-aged lady in a charcoal tailor-made suit, heavily, yet not ungracefully, swinging her hips, made her way amongst the sidewalk tables. There was no vacant one. Finally, she put one hand in a glossy black glove upon the back of the empty chair opposite Erwin.

"May I?" queried her unsmiling eyes from under the short veil of her velvet hat.

"Yes, certainly," answered Erwin slightly rising and ducking. He was not awed by such solid-built women with thickly powdered, somewhat masculine jowls.

Down onto the table with a resolute thud went her over-sized handbag. She ordered a cup of coffee and a wedge of apple tart. Her deep voice was somewhat hoarse but pleasant.

The vast sky, suffused with dull rose, grew darker. A tram screeched by, inundating the asphalt with the radiant tears of its lights. And short-skirted beauties walked by. Erwin's glance followed them.

"I want this one," he thought, notching his nether lip. "And that one, too."

"I think it could be arranged," said his vis-à-vis in the same calm husky tones in which she had addressed the waiter.

Erwin almost fell off his chair. The lady looked intently at him, as she pulled off one glove to tackle her coffee. Her made-up eyes shone cold and hard, like showy false jewels.

Dark pouches swelled under them, and—what seldom occurs in the case of women, even elderly women—hairs grew out of her feline-shaped nostrils. The shed glove revealed a big wrinkled hand with long, convex, beautiful fingernails.

"Don't be surprised," she said with a wry smile. She muffled a yawn and added: "In point of fact, I am the Devil."

Shy, naive Erwin took this to be a figure of speech, but the lady, lowering her voice, continued as follows:

"Those who imagine me with horns and a thick tail are greatly mistaken. Only once did I appear in that shape, to some Byzantine imbecile, and I really don't know why it was such a damned success. I am born three or four times every two centuries. In the eighteen-seventies, some fifty years ago, I was buried, with picturesque honors and a great shedding of blood, on a hill above a cluster of African villages of which I had been ruler. My term there was a rest after more stringent incarnations. Now I am a German-born woman whose last husband—I had, I think, three in all—was of French extraction, a Professor Monde. In recent years I have driven several young men to suicide, caused a well-known artist to copy and multiply the picture of the Westminster Abbey on the pound note, incited a virtuous family man—— But there is really nothing to brag about. This has been a pretty banal avatar, and I am fed up with it."

She gobbled up her slice of tart and Erwin, mumbling something, reached for his hat which had fallen under the table.

"No, don't go yet," said Frau Monde, simultaneously beckoning the waiter. "I am offering you something. I am offering you a harem. And if you are still skeptical of my power——See that old gentleman in tortoise-shell glasses crossing the street? Let's have him hit by a tram."

Erwin, blinking, turned streetward. As the old man reached the tracks he took out his handkerchief and was about to sneeze into it. At the same instant, a tram flashed, screeched, and rolled past. From both sides of the avenue people rushed toward the tracks. The old gentleman, his glasses and handkerchief gone, was sitting on the asphalt. Someone helped him up. He stood, sheepishly shaking his head, brushing his coat sleeves with the palms of his hands, and wiggling one leg to test its condition.

"I said 'hit by a tram,' not 'run over,' which I might also have said," remarked Frau Monde coolly, as she worked a thick cigarette into an enameled holder. "In any case, this is an example."

She blew two streams of gray smoke through her nostrils and again fixed Erwin with her hard bright eyes.

"I liked you immediately. That shyness, that bold imagination. You reminded me of an innocent, though hugely endowed, young monk whom I knew in Tuscany. This is my penultimate night. Being a woman has its points, but being an aging woman is hell, if you will pardon me the expression. Moreover, I made such mischief the other day— you will soon read about it in all the papers—that I had better get out of this life. Next Monday I plan to be born elsewhere. The Siberian slut I have chosen shall be the mother of a marvelous, monstrous man."

"I see," said Erwin.

"Well, my dear boy," continued Frau Monde, demolishing her second piece of pastry, "I intend, before going, to have a bit of innocent fun. Here is what I suggest. Tomorrow, from noon to midnight you can select by your usual method" (with heavy humor Frau Monde sucked in her lower lip with a succulent hiss) "all the girls you fancy. Before my departure, I shall have them gathered and placed at your complete disposal. You will keep them until you have enjoyed them all. How does that strike you, *amico?*"

Erwin dropped his eyes and said softly: "If it is all true, it would be a great happiness."

"All right then," she said, and licked the remains of whipped cream off her spoon: "All right. One condition, nevertheless, must be set. No, it is not what you are thinking. As I told you, I have arranged my next incarnation. *Your* soul I do not require. Now this is the condition: the total of your choices between noon and midnight must be an odd number. This is essential and final. Otherwise I can do nothing for you."

Erwin cleared his throat and asked, almost in a whisper:

"But—how shall I know? Let's say I've chosen one— what then?"

"Nothing," said Frau Monde. "Your feeling, your desire, are a command in themselves. However, in order that you may be sure that the deal stands, I shall have a sign given you every time—a smile, not necessarily addressed to you, a chance word in the crowd, a sudden patch of color—that sort of thing. Don't worry, you'll know."

"And—and—" mumbled Erwin, shuffling his feet under the table: "—and where is it all going to—uh—happen? I have only a very small room."

"Don't worry about that either," said Frau Monde, and her corset creaked as she rose. "Now it's time you went home. No harm in getting a good night's rest. I'll give you a lift."

[46]

In the open taxi, with the dark wind streaming between starry sky and glistening asphalt, poor Erwin felt tremendously elated. Frau Monde sat erect, her crossed legs forming a sharp angle, and the city lights flashed in her gemlike eyes.

"Here's your house," she said, touching Erwin's shoulder. "Au revoir."

3

Many are the dreams that can be brought on by a mug of dark beer laced with brandy. Thus reflected Erwin when he awoke the next morning—he must have been drunk, and the talk with that funny female was all fancy. This rhetorical turn often occurs in fairy tales and, as in fairy tales, our young man soon realized he was wrong.

He went out just as the church clock had begun the laborious task of striking noon. Sunday bells joined in excitedly, and a bright breeze ruffled the Persian lilacs around the public lavatory in the small park near his house. Pigeons settled on an old stone *Herzog* or waddled along the sandbox where little children, their flannel behinds sticking up, were digging with toy scoops and playing with wooden trains. The lustrous leaves of the lindens moved in the wind; their ace-of-spades shadows quivered on the graveled path and climbed in an airy flock the trouser legs and skirts of the strollers, racing up and scattering over shoulders and faces, and once again the whole flock slipped back onto the ground, where, barely stirring, they lay in wait for the next foot passenger. In this variegated setting, Erwin noticed a girl in a white dress who had squatted down to tousle with two fingers a fat shaggy pup with warts on its belly. The inclination of her head bared the back of her neck, revealing the ripple of her vertebrae, the fair bloom, the tender hollow between her shoulder blades, and the sun through the leaves found fiery strands in her chestnut hair. Still playing with the puppy, she half-rose from her haunches and clapped her hands above it. The fat little animal rolled over on the gravel, ran off a few feet and toppled on its side. Erwin sat down on a bench and cast a timid and avid glance at her face.

He saw her so clearly, with such piercing and perfect force of perception, that, it seemed, nothing new about her features might have been disclosed by years of previous intimacy. Her palish lips twitched as if repeating every small soft movement of the puppy; her eyelashes beat so brightly as to look like the raylets of her beaming eyes; but most enchanting, perhaps, was the curve of her cheek, now slightly in profile; that dipping line no words, of course, could describe. She started running, showing nice legs, and the puppy tumbled in her wake like a woolly ball. In sudden awareness of his miraculous might, Erwin caught his breath and awaited the promised signal. At that moment the girl turned her head as she ran and flashed a smile at the plump little creature that could barely keep up with her.

"Number one," Erwin said to himself with unwonted complacency and got up from his bench.

He followed the graveled path with scraping footsteps, in gaudy, reddish-yellow shoes worn only on Sundays. He left the oasis of the diminutive park and crossed over to

A Nursery Tale

Amadeus Boulevard. Did his eyes rove? Oh, they did. But, maybe, because the girl in white had somehow left a sunnier mark than any remembered impression, some dancing blind spot prevented him from finding another sweetheart. Soon, however, the blot dissolved, and near a glazed pillar with the tramway timetable our friend observed two young ladies—sisters, or even twins, to judge by their striking resemblance—who were discussing a streetcar route in vibrant, echoing voices. Both were small and slim, dressed in black silk, with saucy eyes and painted lips.

"That's exactly the tram you want," one of them kept saying.

"Both, please," Erwin requested quickly.

"Yes, of course," said the other in response to her sister's words.

Erwin continued along the boulevard. He knew all the smart streets where the best possibilities existed.

"Three," he said to himself. "Odd number. So far so good. And if it were midnight right now——"

Swinging her handbag she was coming down the steps of the Leilla, one of the best local hotels. Her big blue-chinned companion slowed down behind her to light his cigar. The lady was lovely, hatless, bobhaired, with a fringe on her forehead that made her look like a boy actor in the part of a damsel. As she went by, now closely escorted by our ridiculous rival, Erwin remarked simultaneously the crimson artificial rose in the lapel of her jacket and the advertisement on a billboard: a blond-mustached Turk and, in large letters, the word "Yes!," under which it said in smaller characters: "I smoke only the Rose of the Orient."

That made four, divisible by two, and Erwin felt eager to restore the odd-number rigmarole without delay. In a lane off the boulevard there was a cheap restaurant which he sometimes frequented on Sundays when sick of his landlady's fare. Amongst the girls he had happened to note at one time or another there had been a wench who worked in that place. He entered and ordered his favorite dish: blood sausage and sauerkraut. His table was next to the telephone. A man in a bowler called a number and started to jabber as ardently as a hound that has picked up the scent of a hare. Erwin's glance wandered toward the bar— and there was the girl he had seen three or four times before. She was beautiful in a drab, freckled way, if beauty can be drably russet. As she raised her bare arms to place her washed beer steins he saw the red tufts of her armpits.

"All right, all right!" barked the man into the mouthpiece.

With a sigh of relief enriched by a belch Erwin left the restaurant. He felt heavy and in need of a nap. To tell the truth, the new shoes pinched like crabs. The weather had changed. The air was sultry. Great domed clouds grew and crowded one another in the hot sky. The streets were becoming deserted. One could feel the houses fill to the brim with Sunday-afternoon snores. Erwin boarded a streetcar.

The tram started to roll. Erwin turned his pale face, shining with sweat, to the window but no girls walked. While paying his fare he noticed, on the other side of the aisle a woman sitting with her back to him. She wore a black velvet hat, and a light frock patterned with intertwined chrysanthemums against a semitransparent mauve background through which showed the shoulder straps of her slip. The lady's statuesque bulk made Erwin curious to glimpse her face. When her hat moved and, like a black ship, started to turn, he first looked away as usual, glanced

A Nursery Tale

in feigned abstraction at a youth sitting opposite him, at
his own fingernails, at a red-cheeked little old man dozing
in the rear of the car, and having thus established a point
of departure justifying further castings-around, Erwin
shifted his casual gaze to the lady now looking his way. It
was Frau Monde. Her full, no-longer-young face was
blotchily flushed from the heat, her mannish eyebrows
bristled above her piercing prismatic eyes, a slightly sar-
donic smile curled up the corners of her compressed lips.

"Good afternoon," she said in her soft husky voice:
"Come sit over here. Now we can have a chat. How are
things going?"

"Only five," replied Erwin with embarrassment.

"Excellent. An odd number. I would advise you to stop
there. And at midnight—ah, yes, I don't think I told you—
at midnight you are to come to Hoffmann Street. Know
where that is? Look between Number Twelve and Fourteen. The vacant lot there will be replaced by a villa with
a walled garden. The girls of your choice will be waiting
for you on cushions and rugs. I shall meet you at the garden gate—but it is understood," she added with a subtle
smile, "I shan't intrude. You'll remember the address?
There will be a brand-new streetlight in front of the gate."

"Oh, one thing," said Erwin, collecting his courage. "Let
them be dressed at first—I mean let them look just as they
were when I chose them—and let them be very merry and
loving."

"Why, naturally," she replied, "Everything will be just
as you wish whether you tell me or not. Otherwise there
was no point in starting the whole business, *n'est-ce pas?*
Confess, though, my dear boy—you were on the brink of
enrolling me in your harem. No, no, have no fear, I am

[51]

kidding you. Well, that's your stop. Very wise to call it a day. Five is fine. See you a few secs after midnight, ha-ha."

4

Upon reaching his room, Erwin took off his shoes and stretched out on the bed. He woke up toward evening. A mellifluous tenor at full blast streamed from a neighbor's phonograph: *"I vant to be happee—"*

Erwin started thinking back: "Number one, the Maiden in White, she's the most artless of the lot. I may have been a little hasty. Oh well, no harm done. Then the Twins near the pillar of glass. Gay, painted young things. With them I'm sure to have fun. Then number four, Leilla the Rose, resembling a boy. That's, perhaps, the best one. And finally, the Fox in the ale-house. Not bad either. But only five. That's not very many!"

He lay prone for a while with his hands behind his head, listening to the tenor, who kept wanting to be happy:

"Five. No, that's absurd. Pity it's not Monday morning: those three shopgirls the other day—oh, there are so many more beauties waiting to be found! And I can always throw in a streetwalker at the last moment."

Erwin put on his regular pair of shoes, brushed his hair, and hurried out.

By nine o'clock he had collected two more. One of them he noticed in a café where he had a sandwich and two drams of Dutch gin. She was talking with great animation to her companion, a beard-fingering foreigner, in an impenetrable language—Polish or Russian—and her gray eyes had a slight slant, her thin aquiline nose wrinkled when she laughed, and her elegant legs were exposed to the knee. While Erwin watched her quick gestures, the reckless way in which she tap-tapped cigarette ash all over the table, a German word, like a window, flashed open in her Slavic speech and this chance word (*"offenbar"*) was the "evident" sign. The other girl, number seven, on the list, turned up at the Chinese-style entrance of a small amusement park. She wore a scarlet blouse with a bright-green skirt, and her bare neck swelled as she shrieked in glee, fighting off a couple of slap-happy young boors who were grabbing her by the hips and trying to make her accompany them.

"I'm willing, I'm willing!" she cried out at last, and was rushed away.

Varicolored paper lanterns enlivened the place. A sledge-like affair with wailing passengers hurtled down a serpentine channel, disappeared in the angled arcades of medieval scenery, and dived into a new abyss with new howls. Inside a shed, on four bicycle seats (there were no wheels, just the frames, pedals and handlebars), sat four girls in jerseys and shorts—a red one, a blue one, a green one, a yellow one—their bare legs working at full tilt. Above them hung a dial on which moved four pointers, red, blue, green, and yellow. At first the blue one was first, then the green overtook it. A man with a whistle stood by and collected the coins of the few simpletons who wanted to place their bets. Erwin stared at those magnificent legs, naked nearly up to the groin and pedaling with passionate power.

"They must be terrific dancers," he thought, "I could use all four."

The pointers obediently gathered into one bunch and came to a stop.

"Dead heat!" shouted the man with the whistle. "A sensational finish!"

Erwin drank a glass of lemonade, consulted his watch, and made for the exit.

"Eleven o'clock and eleven women. That will do, I suppose."

He narrowed his eyes as he imagined the pleasures awaiting him. He was glad he had remembered to put on clean underwear.

"How slyly Frau Monde put it," reflected Erwin with a smile. "Of course she will spy on me and why not? It will add some spice."

He walked, looking down, shaking his head delightedly, and only rarely glancing up to check the street names. Hoffmann Street, he knew, was quite far, but he still had an hour, so there was no need to hurry. Again, as on the previous night, the sky swarmed with stars and the asphalt glistened like smooth water, absorbing and lengthening the magic lights of the town. He passed a large cinema whose radiance flooded the sidewalk, and at the next corner a short peal of childish laughter caused him to raise his eyes.

He saw before him a tall elderly man in evening clothes with a little girl walking beside—a child of fourteen or so in a low-cut black party dress. The whole city knew the elderly man from his portraits. He was a famous poet, a senile swan, living all alone in a distant suburb. He strode with a kind of ponderous grace; his hair, the hue of soiled cottonwool, reached over his ears from beneath his fedora. A stud in the triangle of his starched shirt caught the gleam of a lamp, and his long bony nose cast a wedge of shadow on one side of his thin-lipped mouth. In the same tremulous instant Erwin's glance lit on the face of the child mincing at the old poet's side; there was something odd about that face, odd was the flitting glance of her much too shiny eyes, and if she were not just a little girl—the old man's granddaughter, no doubt—one might suspect that her lips were touched up with rouge. She walked swinging her hips very, very slightly, her legs moved close together, she was asking her companion something in a ringing voice—and although Erwin gave no command mentally, he knew that his swift secret wish had been fulfilled.

"Oh, of course, of course," replied the old man coaxingly, bending toward the child.

They passed. Erwin caught a whiff of perfume. He looked back, then went on.

"Heigh, careful," he suddenly muttered as it dawned upon him that this made twelve—an even number: "I must find one more—within half an hour."

It vexed him a little to go on searching but at the same time he was pleased to be given yet another chance.

"I'll pick up one on the way," he said to himself, allaying a trace of panic. "I'm sure to find one!"

"Maybe, it will be the nicest of all," he remarked aloud as he peered into the glossy night.

And a few minutes later he experienced the familiar delicious contraction—that chill in the solar plexus. A woman in front of him was walking along with rapid and light steps. He saw her only from the back and could not have explained why he yearned so poignantly to overtake precisely *her* and have a look at her face. One might, naturally, find random words to describe her bearing, the movement of her shoulders, the silhouette of her hat—but what is the use? Something beyond visible outlines, some kind of special atmosphere, an ethereal excitement, lured Erwin on and on. He marched fast and still could not catch up with her; the humid reflections of lights flickered before him; she tripped along steadily, and her black shadow would sweep up, as it entered a streetlamp's aura, glide across a wall, twist around its edge, and vanish.

"Goodness, I've got to see her face," Erwin muttered. "And time is flying."

Presently he forgot about time. That strange silent chase in the night intoxicated him. He managed at last to overtake her and went on, far ahead, but had not the courage to look back at her and merely slowed down, whereupon she passed him in her turn and so fast that he did not have time to raise his eyes. Again he was walking ten paces behind her and by then he knew, without seeing her face, that she was his main prize. Streets burst into colored light, petered out, glowed again; a square had to be crossed, a space of sleek blackness, and once more with a brief click of her high-heeled shoe the woman stepped onto a sidewalk, with Erwin behind, bewildered, disembodied, dizzy from the misty lights, the damp night, the chase.

What enticed him? Not her gait, not her shape, but something else, bewitching and overwhelming, as if a tense shimmer surrounded her: mere fantasy, maybe, the flutter, the rapture of fantasy, or maybe it was that which changes a man's entire life with one divine stroke—Erwin knew nothing, he just sped after her over asphalt and stone, which seemed also dematerialized in the iridescent night.

Then trees, vernal lindens, joined the hunt: they advanced whispering on either side, overhead, all around him; the little black hearts of their shadows intermingled at the foot of each streetlamp, and their delicate sticky aroma encouraged him.

Once again Erwin came near. One more step, and he would be abreast of her. She stopped abruptly at an iron wicket and fished out her keys from her handbag. Erwin's momentum almost made him bump into her. She turned her face toward him and by the light a streetlamp cast through emerald leaves, he recognized the girl who had been playing that morning with a woolly black pup on a graveled path, and immediately remembered, immediately understood all her charm, tender warmth, priceless radiance.

He stood staring at her with a wretched smile.

"You ought to be ashamed of yourself," she said quietly. "Leave me alone."

The little gate opened, and slammed. Erwin remained standing under the hushed lindens. He looked around, not knowing which way to go. A few paces away, he saw two blazing bubbles: a car standing by the sidewalk. He went up to it and touched the motionless, dummylike chauffeur on the shoulder.

"Tell me what street is this? I'm lost."

"Hoffmann Street," said the dummy dryly.

And then a familiar, husky, soft voice spoke out of the depths of the car.

"Hello. It's me."

Erwin leaned a hand on the car door and limply responded.

"I am bored to death," said the voice, "I'm waiting here for my boyfriend. He is bringing the poison. He and I are dying at dawn. How are you?"

"Even number," said Erwin, running his finger along the dusty door.

"Yes, I know," calmly rejoined Frau Monde. "Number thirteen turned out to be number one. You bungled the job rather badly."

"A pity," said Erwin.

"A pity," she echoed, and yawned.

Erwin bowed, kissed her large black glove, stuffed with five outspread fingers, and with a little cough turned into the darkness. He walked with a heavy step, his legs ached, he was oppressed by the thought that tomorrow was Monday and it would be hard to get up.

MUSIC

Musyka, *a trifle singularly popular with translators, was written at the beginning of 1932, in Berlin. It appeared in the Paris émigré daily* Poslednie Novosti *(March 27, 1932) and in the collection of my stories* Soglyadatay *published by the Russkiya Zapiski firm, in Paris, 1938.*

THE ENTRANCE hall overflowed with coats of both sexes; from the drawing room came a rapid succession of piano notes. Victor's reflection in the hall mirror straightened the knot of a reflected tie. Straining to reach up, the maid hung his overcoat, but it broke loose, taking down two others with it, and she had to begin all over again.

Already walking on tiptoe, Victor reached the drawing room, whereupon the music at once became louder and manlier. At the piano sat Wolf, a rare guest in that house. The rest—some thirty people in all—were listening in a variety of attitudes, some with chin propped on fist, others sending cigarette smoke up toward the ceiling, and the uncertain lighting lent a vaguely picturesque quality to their immobility. From afar, the lady of the house, with an eloquent smile, indicated to Victor an unoccupied seat, a pretzel-backed little armchair almost in the shadow of the grand piano. He responded with self-effacing gestures—it's all right, it's all right, I can stand; presently, however, he began moving in the suggested direction, cautiously sat down, and cautiously folded his arms. The performer's wife, her mouth half-open, her eyes blinking fast, was about to turn the page; now she has turned it. A black forest of ascending notes, a slope, a gap, then a separate group of little trapezists in flight. Wolf had long, fair eyelashes; his translucent ears were of a delicate crimson hue; he struck the keys with extraordinary velocity and vigor and, in the lacquered depths of the open keyboard lid, the doubles of his hands were engaged in a ghostly, intricate, even somewhat clownish mimicry.

To Victor any music he did not know—and all he knew was a dozen conventional tunes—could be likened to the patter of a conversation in a strange tongue: in vain you strive to define at least the limits of the words, but everything slips and merges, so that the laggard ear begins to feel boredom. Victor tried to concentrate on listening, but soon caught himself watching Wolf's hands and their spectral reflections. When the sounds grew into insistent thunder, the performer's neck would swell, his widespread fingers tensed, and he emitted a faint grunt. At one point his wife got ahead of him; he arrested the page with an instant slap of his open left palm, then with incredible speed himself flipped it over, and already both hands were fiercely kneading the compliant keyboard again. Victor made a detailed study of the man: sharp-tipped nose, jutting eyelids, scar left by a boil on his neck, hair resembling blond fluff, broad-shouldered cut of black jacket. For a moment Victor tried to attend to the music again, but scarcely had he focused on it when his attention dissolved. He slowly turned away, fishing out his cigarette case, and began to examine the other guests. Among the strange faces he discovered some familiar ones—nice, chubby Kocharovsky over there —should I nod to him? He did, but overshot his mark: it was another acquaintance, Shmakov, who acknowledged the nod: I heard he was leaving Berlin for Paris—must ask him about it. On a divan, flanked by two elderly ladies, corpulent, red-haired Anna Samoylovna, half-reclined with closed eyes, while her husband, a throat specialist, sat with his elbow propped on the arm of his chair. What is that glittering object he twirls in the fingers of his free hand? Ah yes, a pince-nez on a Chekhovian ribbon. Further, one shoulder in shadow, a hunchbacked, bearded man known to be a lover of music listened intently, an index finger stretched up against his temple. Victor could never remember his name and patronymic. Boris? No, that wasn't it. Borisovich? Not that either. More faces. Wonder if the Haruzins are here. Yes, there they are. Not looking my way. And in the next instant, immediately behind them, Victor saw his former wife.

At once he lowered his gaze, automatically tapping his cigarette to dislodge the ash that had not yet had time to form. From somewhere low down his heart rose like a fist to deliver an uppercut, drew back, struck again, then went into a fast, disorderly throb, contradicting the music and drowning it. Not knowing which way to look, he glanced askance at the pianist, but did not hear a sound: Wolf seemed to be pounding a silent keyboard. Victor's chest got so constricted that he had to straighten up and draw a deep breath; then, hastening back from a great distance, gasping for air, the music returned to life, and his heart resumed beating with a more regular rhythm.

They had separated two years before, in another town, where the sea boomed at night, and where they had lived since their marriage. With his eyes still cast down, he tried to ward off the thunder and rush of the past with trivial thoughts: for instance, that she must have observed him a few moments ago as, with long, noiseless, bobbing strides, he had tiptoed the whole length of the room to reach this

[63]

chair. It was as if someone had caught him undressed or engaged in some idiotic occupation; and, while recalling how in his innocence he had glided and plunged under her gaze (hostile? derisive? curious?), he interrupted himself to consider if his hostess or anyone else in the room might be aware of the situation, and how had she got here, and whether she had come alone or with her new husband, and what he, Victor, ought to do: stay as he was or look her way? No, looking was still impossible; first he had to get used to her presence in this large but confining room— for the music had fenced them in and had become for them a kind of prison, where they were both fated to remain captive until the pianist ceased constructing and keeping up his vaults of sound.

What had he had time to observe in that brief glance of recognition a moment ago? So little: her averted eyes, her pale cheek, a lock of black hair, and, as a vague secondary character, beads or something around her neck. So little! Yet that careless sketch, that half-finished image already *was* his wife, and its momentary blend of gleam and shade already formed the unique entity which bore her name.

How long ago it all seemed! He had fallen madly in love with her one sultry evening, under a swooning sky, on the terrace of the tennis-club pavilion, and, a month later, on their wedding night, it rained so hard you could not hear the sea. What bliss it had been. Bliss—what a moist, lapping and plashing word, so alive, so tame, smiling and crying all by itself. And the morning after: those glistening leaves in the garden, that almost noiseless sea, that languid, milky, silvery sea.

Something had to be done about his cigarette butt. He turned his head, and again his heart missed a beat. Someone had stirred, blocking his view of her almost totally, and was taking out a handkerchief as white as death; but presently the stranger's elbow would go and she would reappear, yes, in a moment she would reappear. No, I can't bear to look. There's an ashtray on the piano.

The barrier of sounds remained just as high and impenetrable. The spectral hands in their lacquered depths continued to go through the same contortions. "We'll be happy forever"—what melody in that phrase, what shimmer! She was velvet-soft all over, one longed to gather her up the way one could gather up a foal and its folded legs. Embrace her and fold her. And then what? What could one do to possess her completely? I love your liver, your kidneys, your blood cells. To this she would reply, "Don't be disgusting." They lived neither in luxury nor in poverty, and went swimming in the sea almost all year round. The jellyfish, washed up onto the shingly beach, trembled in the wind. The Crimean cliffs glistened in the spray. Once they saw fishermen carrying away the body of a drowned man; his bare feet, protruding from under the blanket, looked surprised. In the evenings she used to make cocoa.

He looked again. She was now sitting with downcast eyes, legs crossed, chin propped upon knuckles: she was very musical, Wolf must be playing some famous, beautiful piece. "I won't be able to sleep for several nights," thought Victor as he contemplated her white neck and the soft angle of her knee. She wore a flimsy black dress, unfamiliar to him, and her necklace kept catching the light. "No, I won't be able to sleep, and I shall have to stop coming here. It has all been in vain: two years of straining and struggling, my peace of mind almost regained—now I must start all over again, trying to forget everything, everything that had already been almost forgotten, plus this evening on top of it." It suddenly seemed to him that she was looking at him furtively and he turned away.

The music must be drawing to a close. When they come, those stormy, gasping chords, it usually signifies that the end is near. Another intriguing word, *end* . . . Rend, impend . . . Thunder rending the sky, dust clouds of impending doom. With the coming of spring she became strangely unresponsive. She spoke almost without moving her lips. He would ask "What is the matter with you?" "Nothing. Nothing in particular." Sometimes she would stare at him out of narrowed eyes, with an enigmatic expression. "What *is* the matter?" "Nothing." By nightfall she would be as good as dead. You could not do anything with her, for, despite her being a small, slender woman, she would grow heavy and unwieldy, and as if made of stone. "Won't you finally tell me what is the matter with you?" So it went for almost a month. Then, one morning—yes, it was the morning of her birthday—she said quite simply, as if she were talking about some trifle, "Let's separate for a while. We can't go on like this." The neighbors' little daughter burst into the room to show her kitten (the sole survivor of a litter that had been drowned). "Go away, go away, later." The little girl left. There was a long silence. After a while, slowly, silently, he began twisting her wrists—he longed to break all of her, to dislocate all her joints with loud cracks. She started to cry. Then he sat down at the table and pretended to read the newspaper. She went out into the garden, but soon returned. "I can't keep it back any longer. I have to tell you everything." And with an odd astonishment, as if discussing another woman, and being astonished

[66]

at her, and inviting him to share her astonishment, she told it, told it all. The man in question was a burly, modest, and reserved fellow; he used to come for a game of whist, and liked to talk about artesian wells. The first time had been in the park, then at his place.

The rest is all very vague. I paced the beach till nightfall. Yes, the music does seem to be ending. When I slapped his face on the quay, he said, "You'll pay dearly for this," picked up his cap from the ground, and walked away. I did not say good-bye to her. How silly it would have been to think of killing her. Live on, live. Live as you are living now; as you are sitting now, sit like that forever. Come, look at me, I implore you, please, please look. I'll forgive you everything, because someday we must all die, and then we shall know everything, and everything will be forgiven —so why put it off? Look at me, look at me, turn your eyes, *my* eyes, my darling eyes. No. Finished.

The last many-clawed, ponderous chords—another, and just enough breath left for one more, and, after this concluding chord, with which the music seemed to have surrendered its soul entirely, the performer took aim and, with feline precision, struck one simple, quite separate little golden note. The musical barrier dissolved. Applause. Wolf said, "Its been a very long time since I last played this." Wolf's wife said, "It's been a long time, you know, since my husband last played this piece." Advancing upon him, crowding him, nudging him with his paunch, the throat specialist said to Wolf: "Marvelous! I have always maintained that's the best thing he ever wrote. I think that toward the end you modernize the color of sound just a bit too much. I don't know if I make myself clear, but, you see——"

Victor was looking in the direction of the door. There, a slightly built, black-haired lady with a helpless smile was taking leave of the hostess, who kept exclaiming in surprise, "I won't hear of it, we're all going to have tea now, and then we're going to hear a singer." But she kept on smiling helplessly and made her way to the door, and Victor realized that the music, which before had seemed a narrow dungeon where, shackled together by the resonant sounds, they had been compelled to sit face to face some twenty feet apart, had actually been incredible bliss, a magic glass dome that had embraced and imprisoned him and her, had made it possible for him to breathe the same air as she; and now everything had been broken and scattered, she was disappearing through the door, Wolf had shut the piano, and the enchanting captivity could not be restored.

She left. Nobody seemed to have noticed anything. He was greeted by a man named Boke who said in a gentle voice, "I kept watching you. What a reaction to music! You know, you looked so bored I felt sorry for you. Is it possible that you are so completely indifferent to it?"

"Why, no. I wasn't bored," Victor answered awkwardly. "It's just that I have no ear for music, and that makes me a poor judge. By the way, what was it he played?"

"What you will," said Boke in the apprehensive whisper of a rank outsider. " 'A Maiden's Prayer,' or the 'Kreutzer Sonata.' Whatever you will."

LIK

Lik *was published in the émigré review* Russkiya Zapiski, *Paris, February 1939, and in my third Russian collection* (Vesna v Fialte, *Chekhov House, New York, 1956*). Lik *reflects the miragy Riviera surroundings among which I composed it and attempts to create the impression of a stage performance engulfing a neurotic performer though not quite in the way that the trapped actor expected when dreaming of such an experience.*

The present English translation appeared first in The New Yorker, *October 10, 1964, and was included in* Nabokov's Quartet, *Phaedra Publishers, New York, 1966.*

THERE IS a play of the nineteen-twenties, called *L'Abîme* ("*The Abyss*"), by the well-known French author Suire. It has already passed from the stage straight into the Lesser Lethe (the one, that is, that serves the theater—a stream, incidentally, not quite as hopeless as the main river, and containing a weaker solution of oblivion, so that angling producers may still fish something out many years later). This play—essentially idiotic, even ideally idiotic, or, putting it another way, ideally constructed on the solid conventions of traditional dramaturgy—deals with the torments of a middle-aged, rich, and religious French lady suddenly inflamed by a sinful passion for a young Russian named Igor, who has turned up at her chateau and fallen in love with her daughter Angélique. An old friend of the family, a strong-willed, sullen bigot, conveniently knocked together by the author out of mysticism and lechery, is jealous of the heroine's interest in Igor, while she in turn is jealous of the latter's attentions to Angélique; in a word, it is all very compelling and true to life, every speech bears the trade-mark of a respectable tradition, and it goes without saying that there is not a single jolt of talent to disrupt the ordered course of action, swelling where it ought to swell, and interrupted when necessary by a lyric scene or a shamelessly explanatory dialogue between two old retainers.

The apple of discord is usually an early, sour fruit, and should be cooked. Thus the young man of the play threatens to be somewhat colorless, and it is in a vain attempt to touch him up a little that the author has made him a Russian, with all the obvious consequences of such trickery. According to Suire's optimistic intention, he is an émigré Russian aristocrat, recently adopted by an old lady, the Russian wife of a neighboring landowner. One night, at the height of a thunderstorm, Igor comes knocking at our door, enters, riding crop in hand, and announces in agitation that the pinewood is burning on his benefactress's estate, and that our pinery is also in danger. This affects us less strongly than the visitor's youthful glamour, and we are inclined to sink onto a hassock, toying pensively with our necklace, whereupon our bigot friend observes that the reflection of flames is at times more dangerous than the conflagration itself. A solid, high-quality plot, as you can see, for it is clear at once that the Russian will become a regular caller and, in fact, Act Two is all sunny weather and bright summer clothes.

Judging by the printed text of the play, Igor expresses himself (at least in the first scenes, before the author tires of this) not incorrectly but, as it were, a bit hesitantly, every so often interposing a questioning "I think that is how you say it in French?" Later, though, when the turbulent flow of the drama leaves the author no time for such trifles, all foreign peculiarities of speech are discarded and the young Russian spontaneously acquires the rich vocabulary of a native Frenchman; it is only toward the end, during the lull before the final burst of action, that the playwright remembers with a start the nationality of Igor, whereupon the latter casually addresses these words to the old manservant: *"J'étais trop jeune pour prendre part à la . . . comment dit-on . . . velika voïna . . . grande, grande guerre. . . ."* In all fairness to the author, it is true that, except for this *"velika voïna"* and one modest *"dosvidania,"* he does not abuse his acquaintance with the Russian language, contenting himself with the stage direction "Slavic singsong lends a certain charm to Igor's speech."

In Paris, where the play had great success, Igor was played by François Coulot, and played not badly but for some reason with a strong Italian accent, which he evidently wanted to pass off as Russian, and which did not surprise a single Parisian critic. Afterwards, when the play trickled down into the provinces, this role fell by chance to a real Russian actor, Lik (stage name of Lavrentiy Ivanovich Kruzhevnitsyn), a lean, fair-haired fellow with coffee-dark eyes, who had previously won some fame, thanks to a film in which he did an excellent job in the bit part of a stutterer.

It was hard to say, though, if Lik (the word means "countenance" in Russian and Middle English) possessed genuine theatrical talent or was a man of many indistinct callings who had chosen one of them at random but could just as well have been a painter, jeweler, or ratcatcher. Such a person resembles a room with a number of different doors, among which there is perhaps one that does lead straight into some great garden, into the moonlit depths of a marvelous human night, where the soul discovers the treasure intended for it alone. But, be that as it may, Lik had failed to open *that* door, taking instead the Thespian path, which he followed without enthusiasm, with the absent manner of a man looking for signposts that do not exist but that perhaps have appeared to him in a dream, or can be distinguished in the undeveloped photograph of some other locality that he will never, never visit. On the conventional plane of earthly habitus, he was in his thirties, and so was the century. In elderly people stranded not only outside the border of their country but outside that of their own lives, nostalgia evolves into an extraordinarily complex organ, which functions continuously, and its secretion compensates for all that has been lost; or else it becomes a fatal tumor on the soul that makes it painful to breathe, sleep, and associate with carefree foreigners. In Lik, this memory of Russia remained in the embryonic state, confined to misty childhood recollections, such as the resinous fragrance of the first spring day in the country, or the special shape of the snowflake on the wool of his hood. His parents were dead. He lived alone. There was always something sleazy about the loves and friendships that came his way. Nobody wrote gossipy letters to him, nobody took a greater interest in his worries than he did himself, and there was no one to go and complain to about the undeserved precariousness of his very being when he learned from two doctors, a Frenchman and a Russian, that (like many protagonists) he had an incurable heart ailment—while the streets were virtually swarming with robust oldsters. There seemed to be a certain connection between this illness of his and his fondness for fine, expensive things; he might, for example, spend his last 200 francs on a scarf or a fountain pen, but it always, always happened that the scarf would soon get soiled, the pen broken, despite the meticulous, even pious, care he took of things.

In relation to the other members of the company, which he had joined as casually as a fur doffed by a woman lands on this or that quite anonymous chair, he remained as much a stranger as he had been at the first rehearsal. He had immediately had the feeling of being superfluous, of having usurped someone else's place. The director of the company was invariably friendly toward him, but Lik's hypersensitive soul constantly imagined the possibility of a row—as if at any moment he might be unmasked and accused of something unbearably shameful. The very constancy of the director's attitude he interpreted as the utmost indifference to his work, as though everyone had long since reconciled himself to its hopelessly poor quality—and he was being tolerated merely because there was no convenient pretext for his dismissal.

It seemed to him—and perhaps this was actually so—that to these loud, sleek French actors, interconnected by a network of personal and professional passions, he was as much a chance object as the old bicycle that one of the characters deftly disassembled in the second act; hence, when someone gave him a particularly hearty greeting or offered him a cigarette, he would think that there was some misunderstanding, which would, alas, be resolved in a moment. Because of his illness he avoided drinking, but his absence from friendly gatherings, instead of being attributed to lack of sociability (leading to accusations of haughtiness and thus endowing him with, at least, some semblance of a personality), simply went unnoticed, as if there was no question of its being otherwise; and when they did happen to invite him somewhere, it was always in a vaguely interrogative manner ("Coming with us, or . . . ?")—a manner particularly painful to one who is yearning to be persuaded to come. He understood little of the jokes, allusions, and nicknames that the others bandied about with cryptic gaiety. He almost wished some of the joking were at his expense, but even this failed to happen. At the same time, he rather liked some of his colleagues. The actor who played the bigot was in real life a pleasant fat fellow, who had recently purchased a sports car, about which he would talk to you with genuine inspiration. And the ingénue was most charming, too—dark-haired and slender, with her splendidly bright, carefully made-up eyes—but in daytime hopelessly oblivious of her evening confessions on the stage in the garrulous embrace of her Russian fiancé, to whom she so candidly clung. Lik liked to tell himself that only on the stage did she live her true life, being subject the rest of the time to periodic fits of insanity, during which she no longer recognized him and called herself by a different name. With the leading lady he never exchanged a single word apart from their lines, and when this thickset, tense, handsome woman walked past him in the wings, her jowls shaking, he had the feeling that he was but a piece of scenery, apt to fall flat on the floor if someone brushed against him. It is indeed difficult to say whether it was all as poor Lik imagined or whether these perfectly harmless, self-centered people left him alone simply because he did not seek their company, and did not start a conversation with him just as passengers who have established contact among themselves do not address the foreigner absorbed in his book in a corner of the compartment. But even if Lik did attempt in rare moments of self-confidence to convince himself of the irrationality of his vague torments, the memory of similar torments was too recent, and they were too often repeated in new circumstances, for him to be able to overcome them now. Loneliness as a situation can be corrected, but as a state of mind it is an incurable illness.

Lik

He played his part conscientiously, and, at least as far as accent was concerned, more successfully than his predecessor, since Lik spoke French with a Russian lilt, drawing out and softening his sentences, dropping the stress before their close, and filtering off with excessive care the spray of auxiliary expressions that so nimbly and rapidly fly off a Frenchman's tongue. His part was so small, so inconsequential, in spite of its dramatic impact on the actions of the other characters, that it was not worth pondering over; yet he would ponder, especially at the outset of the tour, and not so much out of love for his art as because the disparity between the insignificance of the role itself and the importance of the complex drama of which he was the prime cause struck him as being a paradox that somehow humiliated him personally. However, although he soon cooled to the possibility of improvements suggested to him by both art and vanity (two things that often coincide), he would hurry on-stage with unchanged, mysterious delight, as though, every time, he anticipated some special reward—in no way connected, of course, with the customary dose of neutral applause. Neither did this reward consist in the performer's inner satisfaction. Rather, it lurked in certain extraordinary furrows and folds that he discerned in the life of the play itself, banal and hopelessly pedestrian as it was, for, like any piece acted out by live people, it gained, God knows whence, an individual soul, and attempted for a couple of hours to exist, to evolve its own heat and energy, bearing no relation to its author's pitiful conception or the mediocrity of the players, but awakening, as life awakes in water warmed by sunlight. For instance, Lik might hope, one vague and lovely night, in the midst of the usual performance, to tread, as it were, on a quicksandy spot; something would give, and he would sink forever in a newborn element, unlike anything known—independently developing the play's threadbare themes in ways altogether new. He would pass irrevocably into this element, marry Angélique, go riding over the crisp heather, receive all the material wealth hinted at in the play, go to live in that castle, and, moreover, find himself in a world of ineffable tenderness—a bluish, delicate world where fabulous adventures of the senses occur, and unheard-of metamorphoses of the mind. As he thought about all this, Lik imagined for some reason that when he died of heart failure—and he would die soon—the attack would certainly come on-stage, as it had been with poor Molière, barking out his dog Latin among the doctors; but that he would not notice his death, crossing over instead into the actual world of a chance play, now blooming anew because of his arrival, while his smiling corpse lay on the boards, the toe of one foot protruding from beneath the folds of the lowered curtain.

At the end of the summer, *The Abyss* and two other plays in the repertory were running at a Mediterranean town. Lik appeared only in *The Abyss,* so between the first performance and the second (only two were scheduled) he had a week of free time, which he did not quite know how to use. What is more, the southern climate did not agree with him; he went through the first performance in a blur of greenhouse delirium, with a hot drop of greasepaint now hanging from the tip of his nose, now scalding his upper lip, and when, during the first intermission, he went out on the terrace separating the back of the theater from an Anglican church, he suddenly felt he would not last out the performance, but would dissolve on the stage amid many-colored exhalations, through which, at the final mortal instant, would flash the blissful ray of another—yes, another life. Nevertheless, he made it to the end somehow or other, even if he did see double from the sweat in his eyes, while the smooth contact of his young partner's cool bare arms agonizingly accentuated the melting state of his palms. He returned to his boardinghouse quite shattered, with aching shoulders and a reverberating pain in the back of his head. In the dark garden, everything was in bloom and smelled of candy, and there was a continuous trilling of crickets, which he mistook (as all Russians do) for cicadas.

His illuminated room was antiseptically white compared to the southern darkness framed in the open window. He crushed a red-bellied drunken mosquito on the wall, then sat for a long time on the edge of the bed, afraid to lie down, afraid of the palpitations. The proximity of the sea whose presence he divined beyond the lemon grove oppressed him, as if this ample, viscously glistening space, with only a membrane of moonlight stretched tight across its surface, was akin to the equally taut vessel of his drumming heart, and, like it, was agonizingly bare, with nothing to separate it from the sky, from the shuffling of human feet and the unbearable pressure of the music playing in a nearby bar. He glanced at the expensive watch on his wrist and noticed with a pang that he had lost the crystal; yes, his cuff had brushed against a stone parapet as he had stumbled uphill a while ago. The watch was still alive, defenseless and naked, like a live organ exposed by the surgeon's knife.

He passed his days in a quest for shade and a longing for coolness. There was something infernal in the glimpses of sea and beach, where bronzed demons basked on the torrid shingle. The sunny side of the narrow streets was so strictly forbidden to him that he would have had to solve intricate route-finding problems if there had been purpose in his wanderings. He had, however, nowhere to go. He strolled aimlessly along the shop fronts, which displayed, among other objects, some rather amusing bracelets of what looked like pink amber, as well as decidedly attractive leather bookmarks and wallets tooled with gilt. He would sink into a chair beneath the orange awning of a café, then go home and lie on his bed—stark naked, dreadfully thin and white—and think about the same things he thought about incessantly.

He reflected that he had been condemned to live on the outskirts of life, that it had always been thus and always would be, and that, therefore, if death did not present him with an exit into true reality, he would simply never come to know life. He also reflected that if his parents were alive instead of having died at the dawn of émigré existence, the fifteen years of his adult life might have passed in the warmth of a family; that, had his destiny been less mobile, he would have finished one of the three gymnasiums he had happened to attend at random points of middle, median, mediocre Europe, and would now have a good, solid job among good, solid people. But, strain his imagination as he might, he could not picture either that job or those people, just as he could not explain to himself why he had studied as a youth at a screen-acting school, instead of taking up music or numismatics, window-washing or bookkeeping. And, as always, from each point of its circumference his thought would follow a radius back to the dark center, to the presentiment of nearing death, for which he, who had accumulated no spiritual treasures, was hardly an interesting prey. Nonetheless, she had apparently determined to give him precedence.

One evening, as he was reclining in a canvas chair on the veranda, he was importuned by one of the pension guests, a loquacious old Russian (who had managed on two occasions already to recount to Lik the story of his life, first in one direction, from the present toward the past, and then in the other, against the grain, resulting in two different lives, one successful, the other not), who, settling himself comfortably and fingering his chin, said: "A friend of mine has turned up here; that is, a 'friend,' *c'est beaucoup dire*— I met him a couple of times in Brussels, that's all. Now, alas, he's a completely derelict character. Yesterday—yes, I think it was yesterday—I happened to mention your name, and he says, 'Why, of course I know him—in fact, we're even relatives.' "

"Relatives?" asked Lik with surprise. "I almost never had any relatives. What's his name?"

"A certain Koldunov—Oleg Petrovich Koldunov. . . . Petrovich, isn't it? Know him?"

"It just can't be!" cried Lik, covering his face with his hands.

"Yes. Imagine!" said the other.

"It can't be," repeated Lik. "You see, I always thought ——. This is awful! You didn't give him my address, did you?"

"I did. I understand, though. One feels disgusted and sorry at the same time. Kicked out of everywhere, embittered, has a family, and so on."

"Listen, do me a favor. Can't you tell him I've left."

"If I see him, I'll tell him. But . . . well, I just happened to run into him down at the port. My, what lovely yachts they have down there. That's what I call fortunate people. You live on the water, and sail wherever you feel like. Champagne, girlies, everything all polished . . ."

And the old fellow smacked his lips and shook his head.

What a mad thing to happen, Lik thought all evening. What a mess. . . . He did not know what had given him the idea that Oleg Koldunov was no longer among the living. It was one of those axioms that the rational mind no longer keeps on active duty, relegating it to the remotest depths of consciousness, so that now, with Koldunov's resurrection, he had to admit the possibility of two parallel lines crossing after all; yet it was agonizingly difficult to get rid of the old concept, embedded in his brain—as if the extraction of this single false notion might vitiate the entire order of his other notions and concepts. And now he simply could not recall what data had led him to conclude that Koldunov had perished, and why, in the past twenty years, there had been such a strengthening in the chain of dim initial information out of which Koldunov's doom had been wrought.

Their mothers had been cousins. Oleg Koldunov was two years his elder; for four years they had gone to the same provincial gymnasium, and the memory of those years had always been so hateful to Lik that he preferred not to recall his boyhood. Indeed, his Russia was perhaps so thickly clouded over for the very reason that he did not cherish any personal recollections. Dreams, however, would still occur even now, for there was no control over them.

Lik

Sometimes Koldunov would appear in person, in his own image, in the surroundings of boyhood, hastily assembled by the director of dreams out of such accessories as a classroom, desks, a blackboard, and its dry, weightless sponge. Besides these down-to-earth dreams there were also romantic, even decadent ones—devoid, that is, of Koldunov's obvious presence but coded by him, saturated with his oppressive spirit or filled with rumors about him, with situations and shadows of situations somehow expressing his essence. And this excruciating Koldunovian décor, against which the action of a chance dream would develop, was far worse than the straightforward dream visitations of Koldunov as Lik remembered him—a coarse, muscular high-school boy, with cropped hair and a disagreeably handsome face. The regularity of his strong features was spoiled by eyes that were set too close together and equipped with heavy, leathery lids (no wonder they had dubbed him "The Crocodile," for indeed there was a certain turbid muddy-Nile quality in his glance).

Koldunov had been a hopelessly poor student; his was that peculiarly Russian hopelessness of the seemingly bewitched dunce as he sinks, in a vertical position, through the transparent strata of several repeated classes, so that the youngest boys gradually reach his level, numb with fear, and then, a year later, leave him behind with relief. Koldunov was remarkable for his insolence, uncleanliness, and savage physical strength; after one had a tussle with him, the room would always reek of the menagerie. Lik, on the other hand, was a frail, sensitive, vulnerably proud boy, and therefore represented an ideal, inexhaustible prey. Koldunov would come flowing over him wordlessly, and industriously torture the squashed but always squirming victim on the floor. Koldunov's enormous, splayed palm would go into an obscene, scooping motion as it penetrated the convulsive, panic-stricken depths it sought. Thereupon he would leave Lik, whose back was covered with chalk dust and whose tormented ears were aflame, in peace for an hour or two, content to repeat some obscenely meaningless phrase, insulting to Lik. Then, when the urge returned, Koldunov would sigh, almost reluctantly, before piling on him again, digging his hornlike nails into Lik's ribs or sitting down for a rest on the victim's face. He had a thorough knowledge of all the bully's devices for causing the sharpest pain without leaving marks, and therefore enjoyed the servile respect of his schoolmates. At the same time he nurtured a vaguely sentimental affection for his habitual patient, making a point of strolling with his arm around the other's shoulders during the class breaks, his heavy, distrait paw palpating the thin collarbone, while Lik tried in vain to preserve an air of independence and dignity. Thus Lik's school days were an utterly absurd and unbearable torment. He was embarrassed to complain to anyone, and his nighttime thoughts of how he would finally kill Koldunov merely drained his spirit of all strength. Fortunately, they almost never met outside of school, although Lik's mother would have liked to establish closer ties with her cousin, who was much richer than she and kept her own horses. Then the Revolution began rearranging the furniture, and Lik found himself in a different city, while fifteen-year-old Oleg, already sporting a mustache and completely brutified, disappeared in the general confusion, and a blissful lull began. It was soon replaced, however, by new, more subtle tortures at the hands of the initial rackmaster's minor successors.

Sad to say, on the rare occasions when Lik spoke of his past, he would publicly recall the presumed deceased with that artificial smile with which we reward a distant time ("Those were the happy days") that sleeps with a full belly in a corner of its evil-smelling cage. Now, however, when Koldunov proved to be alive, no matter what adult arguments Lik invoked, he could not conquer the same sensation of helplessness—metamorphosed by reality but all the more manifest—that oppressed him in dreams when from behind a curtain, smirking, fiddling with his belt buckle, stepped the lord of the dream, a dark, dreadful schoolboy. And, even though Lik understood perfectly well that the real, live Koldunov would not harm him now, the possibility of meeting him seemed ominous, fateful, dimly linked to the whole system of evil, with its premonitions of torment and abuse, so familiar to him.

After his conversation with the old man, Lik decided to stay at home as little as possible. Only three days remained before the last performance, so it was not worth the trouble to move to a different boardinghouse; but he could, for instance, take daylong trips across the Italian border or into the mountains, since the weather had grown much cooler, with a drizzling rain and a brisk wind. Early next morning, walking along a narrow path between flower-hung walls, he saw coming toward him a short, husky man, whose dress in itself differed little from the usual uniform of the Mediterranean vacationer—beret, open-necked shirt, espadrilles —but somehow suggested not so much the license of the season as the compulsion of poverty. In the first instant,

Lik was struck most of all by the fact that the monstrous figure that filled his memory with its bulk proved to be in reality hardly taller than himself.

"Lavrentiy, Lavrusha, don't you recognize me?" Koldunov drawled dramatically, stopping in the middle of the path.

The large features of that sallow face with a rough shadow on its cheeks and upper lip, that glimpse of bad teeth, that large, insolent Roman nose, that bleary, questioning gaze—all of it was Koldunovian, indisputably so, even if dimmed by time. But, as Lik looked, this resemblance noiselessly disintegrated, and before him stood a disreputable stranger with the massive face of a Caesar, though a very shabby one.

"Let's kiss like good Russians," Koldunov said grimly, and pressed his cold, salty cheek for an instant against Lik's childish lips.

"I recognized you immediately," babbled Lik. "Just yesterday I heard about you from What's-His-Name . . . Gavrilyuk."

"Dubious character," interrupted Koldunov. "*Méfie-toi*. Well, well—so here is my Lavrusha. Remarkable! I'm glad. Glad to meet you again. That's fate for you! Remember, Lavrusha, how we used to catch gobies together? As clear as if it happened yesterday. One of my fondest memories. Yes."

Lik knew perfectly well that he had never fished with Koldunov, but confusion, ennui, and timidity prevented him from accusing this stranger of appropriating a nonexistent past. He suddenly felt wiggly and overdressed.

"How many times," continued Koldunov, examining with interest Lik's pale-gray trousers, "how many times during the past years . . . Oh yes, I thought of you. Yes, indeed! And where, thought I, is my Lavrusha? I've told my wife about you. She was once a pretty woman. And what line of work are you in?"

"I'm an actor," sighed Lik.

"Allow me an indiscretion," said Koldunov in a confidential tone. "I'm told that in the United States there is a secret society that considers the word 'money' improper, and if payment must be made, they wrap the dollars in toilet paper. True, only the rich belong—the poor have no time for it. Now, here's what I'm driving at," and, his brows raised questioningly, Koldunov made a vulgar, palpating motion with two fingers and thumb—the feel of hard cash.

"Alas, no!" Lik exclaimed innocently. "Most of the year I'm unemployed, and the pay is miserable."

"I know how it is and understand perfectly," said Koldunov with a smile. "In any case . . . Oh, yes—in any case, there's a project I'd like to discuss with you sometime. You could make a nice little profit. Are you doing anything right now?"

"Well, you see, as a matter of fact, I'm going to Bordighera for the whole day, by bus. . . . And tomorrow . . ."

"What a shame—if you had told me, there's a Russian chauffeur I know here, with a smart private car, and I would have shown you the whole Riviera. You ninny! All right, all right. I'll walk you to the bus stop."

"And anyway I'm leaving for good soon," Lik put in.

"Tell me, how's the family? . . . How's Aunt Natasha?" Koldunov asked absently as they walked along a crowded little street that led down to the seafront. "I see, I see," he nodded at Lik's reply. Suddenly a guilty, demented look passed fleetingly across his evil face. "Listen, Lavrusha," he said, pushing him involuntarily and bringing his face close to Lik's on the narrow sidewalk. "Meeting you is an omen for me. It is a sign that all is not lost yet, and I must admit that just the other day I was thinking that all *was* lost. Do you understand what I am saying?"

"Oh, everybody has such thoughts now and then," said Lik.

They reached the promenade. The sea was opaque and corrugated under the overcast sky, and, here and there near the parapet, the foam had splashed onto the pavement. There was no one about except for a solitary lady in slacks sitting on a bench with an open book in her lap.

"Here, give me five francs and I'll buy you some cigarettes for the trip," Koldunov said rapidly. Taking the money, he added in a different, easy tone, "Look, that's the little wife over there—keep her company for a minute, and I'll be right back."

Lik went up to the blond lady and said with an actor's automatism, "Your husband will be right back and forgot to introduce me. I'm a cousin of his."

At the same moment he was sprinkled by the cool dust of a breaker. The lady looked up at Lik with blue, English eyes, unhurriedly closed her red book, and left without a word.

"Just a joke," said Koldunov, as he reappeared, out of breath. "*Voilà.* I'll take a few for myself. Yes, I'm afraid my little woman has no time to sit on a bench and look at the sea. I implore you, promise me that we'll meet again. Remember the omen! Tomorrow, after tomorrow, whenever you want. Promise me! Wait, I'll give you my address."

Lik

He took Lik's brand-new gilt-and-leather notebook, sat down, bent forward his sweaty, swollen-veined forehead, joined his knees, and not only wrote his address, reading it over with agonizing care, redotting an "i" and underlining a word, but also sketched a street map: so, so, then so. Evidently he had done this more than once, and more than once people had stood him up, using the forgotten address as an excuse; hence he wrote with great diligence and force—a force that was almost incantational.

The bus arrived. "So, I'll expect you!" shouted Koldunov, helping Lik aboard. Then he turned, full of energy and hope, and walked resolutely off along the promenade as if he had some pressing, important business, though it was perfectly obvious that he was an idler, a drunkard, and a boor.

The following day, a Wednesday, Lik took a trip to the mountains, and then spent the greater part of Thursday lying in his room with a bad headache. The performance was that evening, the departure tomorrow. At about six in the afternoon he went out to pick up his watch at the jeweler's and buy some nice white shoes—an innovation he had long wanted to sport in the second act. Separating the bead curtain, he emerged from the shop, shoebox under arm, and ran straight into Koldunov.

Koldunov's greeting lacked the former ardor, and had a slightly derisive note instead. "Oho! You won't wriggle out of it this time," he said, taking Lik firmly by the elbow. "Come on, let's go. You'll see how I live and work."

"I have a performance tonight," Lik objected, "and I'm leaving tomorrow!"

"That's just the point, my friend, that's just the point.

Seize the opportunity! Take advantage of it! There will
never be another chance. The card is trumped! Come on.
Get going."

Repeating disconnected words and imitating with all his
unattractive being the senseless joy of a man who has
reached the borderline, and perhaps even gone beyond it (a
poor imitation, Lik thought vaguely), Koldunov walked
briskly, prodding on his weak companion. The entire company of actors was sitting on the terrace of a corner café,
and, noticing Lik, greeted him with a peripatetic smile that
really did not belong to any one member of the group, but
skittered across the lips of each like an independent spot of
reflected sunlight.

Koldunov led Lik up a crooked little street, mottled here
and there by jaundiced, crooked sunlight. Lik had never
visited this squalid, old quarter. The tall, bare façades of
the narrow houses seemed to lean over the pavement from
either side, with their tops almost meeting; sometimes they
coalesced completely, forming an arch. Repulsive infants
were puttering about by the doorways; black, foul-smelling
water ran down the sidewalk gutter. Suddenly changing
direction, Koldunov shoved him into a shop and, flaunting
the cheapest French slang (in the manner of many Russian
paupers), bought two bottles of wine with Lik's money. It
was evident that he was long since in debt here, and now
there was a desperate glee in his whole bearing and in his
menacing exclamations of greeting, which brought no response whatever from either the shopkeeper or the shopkeeper's mother-in-law, and this made Lik even more
uncomfortable. They walked on, turning into an alley, and
although it had seemed that the vile street they had just
ascended represented the utmost limit of squalor, filth, and

congestion, this passage, with limp wash hanging overhead, managed to embody an even greater dejection. At
the corner of a lopsided little square, Koldunov said that
he would go in first, and, leaving Lik, headed for the black
cavity of an open door. Simultaneously a fair-haired little
boy came dashing out of it, but, seeing the advancing
Koldunov, ran back, brushing against a pail which reacted
with a harsh clink. "Wait, Vasyuk!" shouted Koldunov,
and lumbered into his murky abode. As soon as he entered,
a frenzied female voice issued from within, yelling something in what seemed a habitually overwrought tone, but
then the scream ceased abruptly, and a minute later Koldunov peeped out and grimly beckoned to Lik.

Lik crossed the threshold and immediately found himself
in a low-ceilinged, dark room, whose bare walls, as if distorted by some awful pressure from above, formed incomprehensible curves and corners. The place was crammed
with the dingy stage properties of indigence. The boy of a
moment ago sat on the sagging connubial bed; a huge fair-
haired woman with thick bare feet emerged from a corner
and, without a smile on her bloated pale face (whose
every feature, even the eyes, seemed smudged, by fatigue,
or melancholy, or God knows what), wordlessly greeted
Lik.

"Get acquainted, get acquainted," Koldunov muttered in
derisive encouragement, and immediately set about un-
corking the wine. His wife put some bread and a plate of
tomatoes on the table. She was so silent that Lik began to
doubt whether it had been this woman who had screamed
a moment ago.

She sat down on a bench in the back of the room, busy-
ing herself with something, cleaning something . . . with a

knife over a spread newspaper, it seemed—Lik was afraid to look too closely—while the boy, his eyes glistening, moved over to the wall and, maneuvering cautiously, slipped out into the street. There was a multitude of flies in the room, and with maniacal persistence they haunted the table and settled on Lik's forehead.

"All right, let's have a drink," said Koldunov.

"I can't—I'm not allowed to," Lik was about to object, but instead, obeying the oppressive influence he knew well from his nightmares, he took a swallow—and went into a fit of coughing.

"That's better," said Koldunov with a sigh, wiping his trembling lips with the back of his hand. "You see," he continued, filling Lik's glass and his own, "here's the situation. This is going to be a business talk! Allow me to tell you in brief. At the beginning of summer, I worked for a month or so with some other Russians here, collecting beach garbage. But, as you well know, I am an outspoken man who likes the truth, and when a scoundrel turns up, I come right out and say, 'You're a scoundrel,' and, if necessary, I punch him in the mouth. Well, one day . . ."

And Koldunov began telling, circumstantially, with painstaking repetitions, a dull, wretched episode, and one had the feeling that for a long time his life had consisted of such episodes; that humiliation and failure, heavy cycles of ignoble idleness and ignoble toil, culminating in the inevitable row, had long since become a profession with him. Lik, meanwhile, began to feel drunk after the first glass, but nevertheless went on sipping, with concealed revulsion. A kind of tickling fog permeated every part of his body, but he dared not stop, as if his refusal of wine would lead to a shameful punishment. Leaning on one elbow, Koldunov talked uninterruptedly, stroking the edge of the table with one hand and occasionally slapping it to stress some particularly somber word. His head, the color of yellowish clay (he was almost completely bald), the bags under his eyes, the enigmatically malignant expression of his mobile nostrils—all of this had completely lost any connection with the image of the strong, handsome schoolboy who used to torment Lik, but the coefficient of nightmare remained unchanged.

"There you are, friend. . . . This is no longer important," said Koldunov in a different, less narrative tone. "Actually, I had this little tale all ready for you last time, when it occurred to me that fate—I'm an old fatalist—had given a certain meaning to our meeting, that you had come as a savior, so to speak. But now it turns out that, in the first place, you—forgive me—are as stingy as a Jew and, in the second place . . . Who knows, maybe you really are not in a position to make me a loan. . . . Have no fear, have no fear. . . . This topic is closed! Moreover, it would have only been a question of a small sum to get me back not on my feet—that would be a luxury—but merely on all fours. Because I'm sick of sprawling with my face in the muck. I'm not going to ask anything of you; it's not my style to beg. All I want is your opinion, about something. It's merely a philosophical question. Ladies need not listen. How do you explain all this? You see, if a definite explanation exists, then fine, I'm willing to put up with the muck, since that means there is something logical and justified in all this, perhaps something useful to me or to others, I don't know. Here, explain this to me: I am a human being—you certainly cannot deny that, can you? All right. I am a human being, and the same blood runs in my veins as in yours. Believe it or not, I was my late mama's only and beloved. As a boy, I played pranks; as a youth, I went to war, and the ball started rolling—God, how it rolled! What went wrong? No, you tell *me*—what went wrong? I just want to know what went wrong, then I'll be satisfied. Why has life systematically baited me? Why have I been assigned the part of some kind of miserable scoundrel who is spat on by everybody, gypped, bullied, thrown into jail? Here's an example for you: When they were taking me away after a certain incident in Lyon—and I might add that I was absolutely in the right, and am now very sorry I did not finish him off—well, as the police were taking me away, ignoring my protests, you know what they did? They stuck a little hook right here in the live flesh of my neck—what kind of treatment is that, I ask you?—and off the cop led me to the police station, and I floated along like a sleepwalker, because every additional motion made me black out with pain. Well, can you explain why they don't do this to other people and then, all of a sudden, do it to me? Why did my first wife run away with a Circassian? Why did seven people nearly beat me to death in Antwerp in '32, in a small room? And look at all this—what's the reason for it?—these rags, these walls, that Katya over there? . . . The story of my life interests me, and has so for a long while! This isn't any Jack London or Dostoyevski story for you! I live in a corrupt country—all right. I am willing to put up with the French. All right! But we must find some explanation, gentlemen! I was talking with a guy once, and he asks me, 'Why don't you go back to Russia?' Why not, after all? The difference is very small! There they'd persecute me just the same, knock my teeth in, stick me in the cooler, and then invite me to be shot—and at least that would be honest. You see, I'm even willing to respect them —God knows, they are honest murderers—while here these crooks will think up such tortures for you, it's almost enough to make you feel nostalgic for the good old Russian bullet. Hey, why aren't you looking at me—you, you, you—or don't you understand what I'm saying?"

"No, I understand everything," said Lik. "Only please excuse me. I don't feel well, I must be going. I have to be at the theater soon."

"Oh, no. Wait just a minute. I understand a few things myself. You're a strange fellow. . . . Come on, make me an offer of some kind. . . . Try! Maybe you'll shower me with gold after all, eh? Listen, you know what? I'll sell you a gun—it'll be very useful to you on the stage: bang, and down goes the hero. It's not even worth a hundred francs, but I need more than a hundred—I'll let you have it for a thousand. Want it?"

"No, I don't," said Lik listlessly. "And I really have no money. I've been through it all myself, the hunger and so forth. . . . No, I won't have any more, I feel sick."

"You keep drinking, you son of a bitch, and you won't feel sick. All right, forget it. I just did it to see what you'd say—I won't be bought anyway. Only, please answer my question. Who was it decided I should suffer, and then condemned my child to the same lousy Russian fate? Just a minute, though—suppose I, too, want to sit down in my dressing gown and listen to the radio? What went wrong, eh? Take you, for instance—what makes you better than me? You go swaggering around, living in hotels, smooching with actresses. . . . What's the reason for it? Come on, explain it to me."

Lik said, "I turned out to have—I happened to have . . .

Oh, I don't know . . . a modest dramatic talent, I suppose you could say."

"Talent?" shouted Koldunov. "I'll show you talent! I'll show you such talent that you'll start cooking applesauce in your pants! You're a dirty rat, chum. That's your only talent. I must say that's a good one!" (Koldunov started shaking in very primitive mimicry of side-splitting laughter.) "So, according to you, I'm the lowest, filthiest vermin and deserve my rotten end? Splendid, simply splendid. Everything is explained—eureka, eureka! The card is trumped, the nail is in, the beast is butchered!"

"Oleg Petrovich is upset—maybe you ought to be going now," Koldunov's wife suddenly said from her corner, with a strong Estonian accent. There was not the least trace of emotion in her voice, causing her remark to sound wooden and senseless. Koldunov slowly turned in his chair, without altering the position of his hand, which lay as if lifeless on the table, and fixed his wife with an enraptured gaze.

"I am not detaining anyone," he spoke softly and cheerfully. "And I'll be thankful not to be detained by others. Or told what to do. So long, mister," he added, not looking at Lik, who for some reason found it necessary to say:

"I'll write from Paris, without fail. . . ."

"So he's going to write, is he?" said Koldunov softly, apparently still addressing his wife. With some trouble Lik extricated himself from the chair and started in her direction, but swerved and bumped into the bed.

"Go away, it's all right," she said calmly, and then, with a polite smile, Lik stumbled out of the house.

His first sensation was one of relief. He had escaped from the orbit of that drunken, moralizing moron. Then came a mounting horror: he was sick to his stomach, and his arms and legs belonged to different people. How was he to perform that night? The worst of all, though, was that his whole body, which seemed to consist of ripples and dots, sensed the approach of a heart attack. It was as if an invisible stake were pointing at him and he might impale himself any moment. This was why he must follow a weaving course, even stopping and backing slightly now and then. Nevertheless, his mind remained rather lucid, he knew that only thirty-six minutes remained before the start of the performance, and he knew the way home. . . . It would be a better idea, though, to go down to the embankment, to sit by the sea until he felt better. This will pass, this will pass, if only I don't die. . . . He also grasped the fact that the sun had just set, that the sky was already more luminous and more tender than the earth. What unnecessary, offensive nonsense. He walked, calculating every step, but sometimes he would err and passersby would turn to look at him. Happily, he did not encounter many of them, since it was the hallowed dinner hour, and when he reached the seafront, he found it quite deserted; the lights burned on the pier, casting long reflections on the tinted water, and these bright dots and inverted exclamation marks seemed to be shining translucently in his own head. He sat down on a bench, hurting his coccyx as he did so, and shut his eyes. But then everything began to spin; his heart was reflected as a terrifying globe on the dark inner side of his eyelids. It continued to swell agonizingly, and, to put a stop to this, he opened his eyes and tried to hook his gaze on things—on the evening star, on that black buoy in the sea, on a darkened eucalyptus tree at the end of the promenade. I know all this, he thought, I understand all this, and, in the twilight, the eucalyptus strangely resembles a big Russian birch. Can this be the end? Such an idiotic end. . . . I feel worse and worse. . . . What's happening to me? . . . Oh my God!

About ten minutes passed, no more. His watch ticked on, trying tactfully not to look at him. The thought of death coincided precisely with the thought that in half an hour he would walk out onto the bright stage and say the first words of his part, "*Je vous prie d'excuser, Madame, cette invasion nocturne.*" And these words, clearly and elegantly engraved in his memory, seemed far more real than the lapping and splashing of the weary waves, or the sound of two gay female voices coming from behind the stone wall of a nearby villa, or the recent talk of Koldunov, or even the pounding of his own heart. His feeling of sickness suddenly reached such a panicky pitch that he got up and walked along the parapet, dazedly stroking it and peering at the colored inks of the evening sea. "In any case," Lik said aloud, "I have to cool off. . . . Instant cure. . . . Either I'll die or it'll help." He slid down the sloping edge of the sidewalk, where the parapet stopped, and crunched across the pebbly beach. There was nobody on the shore except for a shabbily dressed man, who happened to be lying supine near a boulder, his feet spread wide apart. Something about the outline of his legs and shoulders for some reason reminded Lik of Koldunov. Swaying a little and already stooping, Lik walked self-consciously to the edge of the water, and was about to scoop some up in his hands and douse his head; but the water was alive, moving, and threatening to soak his feet. Perhaps I have enough coordination left to take off my shoes and socks, he thought, and in the same instant remembered the carton box containing his new shoes. He had forgotten it at Koldunov's!

And as soon as he remembered it, this image proved so stimulating that immediately everything was simplified, and this saved Lik, in the same way as a situation is sometimes saved by its rational formulation. He must get those shoes at once, there was just time enough to get them, and as soon as this was accomplished, he would step onstage in them. (All perfectly clear and logical.) Forgetting the pressure in his chest, the foggy feeling, the nausea, Lik climbed back up to the promenade, and in a sonorously recorded voice hailed the empty taxi that was just leaving the curb by the villa across the way. Its brakes responded with a lacerating moan. He gave the chauffeur the address from his notebook, telling him to go as fast as possible, even though the entire trip—there and from there to the theater —would not take more than five minutes.

The taxi approached Koldunov's place from the direction of the square. A crowd had gathered, and it was only by dint of persistent threats with its horn that the driver managed to squeeze through. Koldunov's wife was sitting on a chair by the public fountain. Her forehead and left cheek glistened with blood, her hair was matted, and she sat quite straight and motionless, surrounded by the curious, while, next to her, also motionless, stood her boy, in a bloodstained shirt, covering his face with his fist, a kind of tableau. A policeman, mistaking Lik for the doctor, escorted him into the room. The dead man lay on the floor amid broken crockery, his face blasted by a gunshot in the mouth, his widespread feet in new, white—

"Those are mine," said Lik in French.

RECRUITING

Nabor *was written in the summer of 1935 in Berlin. It appeared on August 18 of that year in the* Poslednie Novosti, *Paris, and was included twenty-one years later in my* Vesna v Fialte *collection, published by the Chekhov House in New York.*

HE WAS old, he was ill, and nobody in the world needed him. In the matter of poverty Vasiliy Ivanovich had reached the point where a man no longer asks himself on what he will live tomorrow, but merely wonders what he had lived on the day before. In the way of private attachments, nothing on this earth meant much to him apart from his illness. His elder, unmarried sister, with whom he had migrated from Russia to Berlin in the 1920s, had died ten years ago. He no longer missed her, having got used instead to a void shaped in her image. That day however, in the tram, as he was returning from the Russian cemetery where he had attended Professor D.'s funeral, he pondered with sterile dismay the state of abandon into which her grave had fallen: the paint of the cross had peeled here and there, the name was barely distinguishable from the linden's shade that glided across it, erasing it. Professor D.'s funeral was attended by a dozen or so resigned old émigrés, linked up by death's shame and its vulgar equality. They stood, as happens in such cases, both singly and together, in a kind of grief-stricken expectation, while the humble ritual, punctuated by the secular stir of the boughs overhead, ran its course. The sun's heat was unbearable, especially on an empty stomach; yet, for the sake of decency, he had worn an overcoat to conceal the meek disgrace of his suit. And even though he had known Professor D. rather well, and tried to hold squarely and firmly before his mind's eye the kindly image of the deceased, in this warm, joyous July wind, which was already rippling and curling it, and tearing it out of his grasp, his thoughts nevertheless kept slipping off into that corner of his memory where, with her inalterable habits, his sister was matter-of-factly returning from the dead, heavy and corpulent like him, with spectacles of identical prescription on her quite masculine, massive, red, seemingly varnished nose, and dressed in a gray jacket such as Russian ladies active in social politics wear to this day: a splendid, splendid soul, living, at first sight, wisely, ably, and briskly but, strangely enough, revealing wonderful vistas of melancholy which only he noticed, and for which, in the final analysis, he loved her as much as he did.

In the impersonal Berlin crush of the tram, there was another old refugee staying around to the very last, a nonpractising lawyer, who was also returning from the cemetery and was also of little use to anyone except me. Vasiliy Ivanovich, who knew him only slightly, tried to decide whether or not to start a conversation with him if the shifting jumble of the tram's contents happened to unite them; the other, meanwhile, remained glued to the window, observing the evolutions of the streets with an ironic expression on his badly neglected face. Finally (and *that* was the very moment I caught, after which I never let the recruit out of my sight), V.I. got off and, since he was heavy and clumsy, the conductor helped him clamber down onto the oblong stone island of the stop. Once on the ground, he accepted from above, with unhurried gratitude, his own arm, which the conductor had still been holding by the sleeve. Then he slowly shifted his feet, turned, and, looking warily around, made for the asphalt with the intention of crossing the perilous street toward a public garden.

He crossed safely. A little while ago, in the churchyard, when the tremulous old priest proposed, according to the ritual, that the choir sing to the eternal memory of the deceased, it took V.I. such a long time and such effort to kneel that the singing was over by the time his knees communicated with the ground, whereupon he could not rise again; old Tihotsky helped him up as the tram conductor had just helped him down. These twin impressions increased a sense of unusual fatigue, which, no doubt, already smacked of the ultimate glebe, yet was pleasant in its own way; and, having decided that in any case it was still too early to head for the apartment of the good, dull people who boarded him, V.I. pointed out a bench to himself with his cane and slowly, not yielding to the force of gravity until the last instant, finally sat down in surrender.

I would like to understand, though, whence comes this happiness, this swell of happiness, that immediately transforms one's soul into something immense, transparent and precious. After all, just think, here is a sick old man with the mark of death already on him; he has lost all his loved ones: his wife, who, when they were still in Russia, left him for Dr. Malinovski, the well-known reactionary; the newspaper where V.I. had worked; his reader, friend, and namesake, dear Vasiliy Ivanovich Maler, tortured to death by the Reds in the Civil War years; his brother, who died of cancer in Kharbin; and his sister.

Once again he thought with dismay about the blurred cross of her grave, which was already creeping over into nature's camp; it must have been seven years or so since he had stopped taking care of it and let it go free. With striking vividness V.I. suddenly pictured a man his sister had once loved—the only man she had ever loved—a Garshin-like character, a half-mad, consumptive, fascinating man, with a coal-black beard and Gypsy eyes, who unexpectedly shot himself because of another woman: that blood on his dickey, those small feet in smart shoes. Then, with no connection at all, he saw his sister as a schoolgirl, with her new little head, shorn after she had had typhoid fever, explaining to him, as they sat on the ottoman, a complex system of tactile perception she had evolved, so that her life turned into a constant preoccupation with maintaining a mysterious equilibrium between objects: touch a wall in passing, a gliding stroke with the left palm, then the right, as if immersing one's hands in the sensation of the object, so that they be clean, at peace with the world and reflected in it; subsequently she was interested mainly in feminist questions, organized women's pharmacies of some kind or other, and had an insane terror of ghosts, because, as she said, she did not believe in God.

Thus, having lost this sister, whom he had loved with special tenderness for the tears she shed at night; back from the cemetery, where the ridiculous rigmarole with spadefuls of earth had revived those recollections; heavy, feeble, and awkward to such an extent that he could not get up off his knees or descend from the platform of the tram (the charitable conductor had to stoop with downstretched hands—and one of the other passengers helped too, I think); tired, lonely, fat, ashamed, with all the nuances of old-fashioned modesty, of his mended linen, his decaying trousers, his whole unkempt, unloved, shabbily furnished corpulence, V.I. nevertheless found himself filled with an almost indecent kind of joy of unknown origin, which, more than once in the course of his long and rather arduous life, had surprised him by its sudden onset. He sat quite still, his hands resting (with only an occasional spreading out of the fingers) on the crook of his cane and his broad thighs parted so that the rounded base of his belly, framed in the opening of his unbuttoned overcoat, reposed on the edge of the bench. Bees were ministering to the blooming linden tree overhead; from its dense festive foliage floated a clouded, melleous aroma, while underneath, in its shadow, along the sidewalk, lay the bright yellow debris of lime flowers, resembling ground-up horse dung. A wet red hose lay across the entire lawn in the center of the small public garden and, a little way off, radiant water gushed from it, with a ghostly iridescence in the aura of its spray. Between some hawthorn bushes and a chalet-style public toilet a dove-gray street was visible; there, a morris pillar covered with posters stood like a fat harlequin, and tram after tram passed with a clatter and whine.

This little street garden, these roses, this greenery—he had seen them a thousand times, in all their uncomplicated transformations, yet it all sparkled through and through with vitality, novelty, participation in one's destiny, whenever he and I experienced such fits of happiness. A man with the local Russian newspaper sat down on the same dark-blue, sun-warmed, hospitable, indifferent bench. It is difficult for me to describe this man; then again, it would be useless, since a self-portrait is seldom successful, because of a certain tension that always remains in the expression of the eyes—the hypnotic spell of the indispensable mirror. Why did I decide that the man next to whom I had sat down was named Vasiliy Ivanovich? Well, because that blend of name and patronymic is like an armchair, and he was broad and soft, with a large cozy face, and sat, with his hands resting on his cane, comfortably and motionlessly; only the pupils of his eyes shifted to and fro, behind their lenses, from a cloud traveling in one direction to a truck traveling in the other, or from a female sparrow feeding her fledgling on the gravel to the intermittent, jerky motion of a little wooden automobile pulled on a string by a child who had forgotten all about it (there—it fell on its side, but nevertheless kept progressing). Professor D.'s obituary occupied a prominent place in the paper, and that is how, in my hurry to give V.I.'s morning some sort of setting as gloomy and typical as possible, I happened to arrange for him that trip to the funeral, even though the paper said there would be a special announcement of the date; but, I repeat, I was in a hurry, and I did wish he had really been to the cemetery, for he was exactly the type you see at Russian ceremonies abroad, standing to one side as it were, but emphasizing by this the habitual nature of his presence; and, since something about the soft features of his full, cleanshaven face reminded me of a Moscow sociopolitical lady named Anna Aksakov, whom I remembered since childhood (she was a distant relative of mine), almost inadvertently but already with irrepressible detail, I made her his sister, and it all happened with vertiginous speed, because at all costs I had to have somebody like him for an episode in a novel with which I have been struggling for more than two years. What did I care if this fat old gentleman, whom I first saw being lowered from the tram, and who was now sitting beside me, was perhaps not Russian at all? I was so pleased with him! He was so capacious! By an odd combination of emotions I felt I was infecting that stranger with the blazing creative happiness that sends a chill over an artist's skin. I wished that, despite his age, his indigence, the tumor in his stomach, V.I. might share the terrible power of my bliss, redeeming its unlawfulness with his complicity, so that it would cease being a unique sensation, a most rare variety of madness, a monstrous sunbow spanning my whole inner being, and be accessible to two people at least, becoming their topic of conversation and thus acquiring rights to routine existence, of which my wild, savage, stifling happiness is otherwise deprived. Vasiliy Ivanovich (I persisted in this appellation) took off his black fedora, as if not in order to refresh his head but with the precise intention of greeting my thoughts. He slowly stroked the crown of his head; the shadows of the linden leaves passed across the veins of his large hand and fell anew on his grayish hair. Just as slowly, he turned his head toward me, glanced at my émigré paper, at my face which was made up to look like that of a reader, turned away majestically, and put his hat on again.

But he was already mine. Presently, with an effort, he got up, straightened, transferred his cane from one hand to the other, took a short, tentative step, and then calmly moved off, forever, if I am not mistaken. Yet he carried off with him, like the plague, an extraordinary disease, for he was sacramentally bound to me, being doomed to appear for a moment in the far end of a certain chapter, at the turning of a certain sentence.

My representative, the man with the Russian newspaper, was now alone on the bench and, as he had moved over into the shade where V.I. had just been sitting, the same cool linden pattern that had anointed his predecessor now rippled across his forehead.

TERROR

Uzhas was written in Berlin, around 1926, one of the happiest years of my life. The Sovremennya Zapiski, the Paris émigré magazine, published it in 1927 and it was included in the first of my three collections of Russian stories, Vozvrashchenie Chorba, Slovo, Berlin, 1930. It preceded Sartre's La Nausée, with which it shares certain shades of thought, and none of that novel's fatal defects, by at least a dozen years.

HERE IS what sometimes happened to me: after spending the first part of the night at my desk—that part when night trudges heavily uphill—I would emerge from the trance of my task at the exact moment when night had reached the summit and was teetering on that crest, ready to roll down into the haze of dawn; I would get up from my chair, feeling chilly and utterly spent, turn on the light in my bedroom, and suddenly see myself in the looking glass. Then it would go like this: during the time I had been deep at work, I had grown disacquainted with myself, a sensation akin to what one may experience when meeting a close friend after years of separation: for a few empty, lucid, but numb moments you see him in an entirely different light even though you realize that the frost of this mysterious anesthesia will presently wear off, and the person you are looking at will revive, glow with warmth, resume his old place, becoming again so familiar that no effort of the will could possibly make you recapture that fleeting sensation of estrangedness. Precisely thus I now stood considering my own reflection in the glass and failing to recognize it as mine. And the more keenly I examined my face—those unblinking alien eyes, that sheen of tiny hairs along the jaw, that shade along the nose—and the more insistently I told myself "This is I, this is so-and-so," the less clear it became *why* this should be "I," the harder I found it to make the face in the mirror merge with that "I" whose identity I failed to grasp. When I spoke of my odd sensations, people justly observed that the path I had taken led to the madhouse. In point of fact, once or twice, late at night, I peered so lengthily at my reflection that a creepy feeling came over me and I put out the light in a hurry. Yet next morning, while shaving, it would never occur to me to question the reality of my image.

Another thing: at night, in bed, I would abruptly remember that I was mortal. What then took place within my mind was much the same as happens in a huge theater if the lights suddenly go out, and someone shrilly screams in the swift-winged darkness, and other voices join in, resulting in a blind tempest, with the black thunder of panic growing—until suddenly the lights come on again, and the performance of the play is blandly resumed. Thus would my soul choke for a moment while, lying supine, eyes wide open, I tried with all my might to conquer fear, rationalize death, come to terms with it on a day-by-day basis, without appealing to any creed or philosophy. In the end, one tells oneself that death is still far away, that there will be plenty of time to reason everything out, and yet one knows that one never will do it, and again, in the dark, from the cheapest seats, in one's private theater where warm live thoughts about dear earthly trifles have panicked, there comes a shriek—and presently subsides when one turns over in bed and starts to think of some different matter.

I assume that those sensations—the perplexity before the mirror at night or the sudden pang of death's foretaste—are familiar to many, and if I dwell on them it is only because they contain just a small particle of that supreme terror that I was destined once to experience. Supreme terror, special terror—I am groping for the exact term but my store of ready-made words, which in vain I keep trying on, does not contain even one that will fit.

I led a happy life. I had a girl. I remember well the torture of our first separation. I had gone on a business trip abroad, and upon my return she met me at the station. I saw her standing on the platform, caged as it were in tawny sunlight, a dusty cone of which had just penetrated through the station's glazed vault. Her face kept rhythmically turning to and fro as the train windows slowly glided by to a stop. With her I always felt easy and at rest. Once only—and here again I feel what a clumsy instrument human speech is. Still, I would like to explain. It is really such nonsense, so ephemeral: we are alone in her room, I write while she darns a silk stocking stretched taut over the back of a wooden spoon, her head bent low; one ear, translucently pink, is half concealed by a strand of fair hair, and the small pearls around her neck gleam touchingly, and her tender cheek appears sunken because of the assiduous pout of her lips. All at once, for no reason at all, I become terrified of her presence. This is far more terrifying than the fact that somehow, for a split second, my mind did not register her identity in the dusty sun of the station. I am terrified by there being another person in the room with me; I am terrified by the very notion of *another person.* No wonder lunatics don't recognize relatives. But she raises her head, all her features participate in the quick smile she gives me—and no trace is left now of the odd terror I felt a moment ago. Let me repeat: this happened only one single time, and I took it to be a silly trick of my nerves, forgetting that on lonely nights before a lonely mirror I had experienced something quite similar.

She was my mistress for nearly three years. I know that many people could not understand our relationship. They were at a loss to explain what there was in that naive little maiden to attract and hold a poet's affection, but good God! how I loved her unassuming prettiness, gaiety, friendliness, the birdlike flutterings of her soul. It was exactly that gentle simplicity of hers that protected me: to her, everything in the world had a kind of everyday clarity, and it would even seem to me that she knew what awaited us after death, so that there was no reason for us to discuss that topic. At the end of our third year together I again was obliged to go away, for a rather long time. On the eve of my departure we went to the opera. She sat down for a moment on the crimson little sofa in the darkish, rather mysterious vestibule of our loge to take off her huge gray snowboots, from which I helped her to extricate her slender silk-clad legs—and I thought of those delicate moths that hatch from bulky shaggy cocoons. We moved to the front of our box. We were gay as we bent over the rosy abyss of the house while waiting for the raising of the curtain, a solid old screen with pale-gold decorations depicting scenes from various operas—Ruslan in his pointed helmet, Lenski in his carrick. With her bare elbow she almost knocked down from the plush parapet her little nacreous opera glass.

Then, when all in the audience had taken their seats, and the orchestra drew in its breath and prepared to blast forth, something happened: every light went out in the huge rosy theater, and such a dense darkness swooped upon us that I thought I had gone blind. In this darkness everything at once began to move, a shiver of panic began to rise and resolved itself in feminine cries, and because men's voices very loudly called for calm, the cries became more and more riotous. I laughed and began talking to her but then felt that she had clutched my wrist and was silently worrying my cuff. When light again filled the house I saw that she was pale and that her teeth were clenched. I helped her to get out of the loge. She shook her head, chiding herself with a deprecatory smile for her childish fright—but then burst into tears and asked to be taken home. It was only in the close carriage that she regained her composure and, pressing her crumpled handkerchief to her swimming bright eyes, began to explain how sad she felt about my going away tomorrow, and how wrong it would have been to spend our last evening at the opera, among strangers.

Twelve hours later I was in a train compartment, looking out of the window at the misty winter sky, the inflamed little eye of the sun, which kept up with the train, the white snow-covered fields which kept endlessly opening up like a giant fan of swan's down. It was in the foreign city I reached next day that I was to have my encounter with supreme terror.

To begin with, I slept badly for three nights in a row and did not sleep at all during the fourth. In recent years I had lost the habit of solitude, and now those solitary nights caused me acute unrelieved anguish. The first night I saw my girl in dream: sunlight flooded her room, and she sat on the bed wearing only a lacy nightgown, and laughed, and laughed, could not stop laughing. I recalled my dream quite by accident, a couple of hours later, as I was passing a lingerie store, and upon remembering it realized that all that had been so gay in my dream—her lace, her thrown-back head, her laughter—was now, in my waking state, frightening. Yet, I could not explain to myself why that lacy laughing dream was now so unpleasant, so hideous. I had a lot of things to take care of, and I smoked a lot, and all the time I was aware of the feeling that I absolutely must maintain rigid control over myself. When getting ready for bed in my hotel room, I would deliberately whistle or hum but would start like a fearful child at the slightest noise behind me, such as the flop of my jacket slipping from the chairback to the floor.

On the fifth day, after a bad night, I took time out for a stroll. I wish the part of my story to which I am coming now could be set in italics; no, not even italics would do: I need some new, unique kind of type. Insomnia had left me with an exceptionally receptive void within my mind. My head seemed made of glass, and the slight cramp in my calves had also a vitreous character. As soon as I came out of the hotel—— Yes, now I think I have found the right words. I hasten to write them down before they fade. When I came out on the street, I suddenly saw the world such as it really *is*. You see, we find comfort in telling ourselves that the world could not exist without us, that it exists only inasmuch as we ourselves exist, inasmuch as we can represent it to ourselves. Death, infinite space, galaxies, all this is frightening, exactly because it transcends the limits of our perception. Well—on that terrible day when, devastated by a sleepless night, I stepped out into the center of an incidental city, and saw houses, trees, automobiles, people, my mind abruptly refused to accept them as "houses," "trees," and so forth—as something connected with ordinary human life. My line of communication with the world snapped, I was on my own and the world was on *its* own, and *that* world was devoid of sense. I saw the actual essence of all things. I looked at houses and they had lost their usual meaning—that is, all that we think when looking at a house: a certain architectural style, the sort of rooms inside, ugly house, comfortable house—all this had evaporated, leaving nothing but an absurd shell the same way an absurd sound is left after one has repeated sufficiently long the commonest word without heeding its meaning: house, howss, whowss. It was the same with trees, the same with people. I understood the horror of a human face. Anatomy, sexual distinctions, the notion of "legs," "arms," "clothes"—all that was abolished, and there remained in front of me a mere *something*—not even a creature, for that too is a human concept, but merely *something* moving past. In vain did I try to master my terror by recalling how once in my childhood, on waking up, I raised my still sleepy eyes while pressing the back of my neck to my low pillow and saw, leaning toward me over the bed head, an incomprehensible face, noseless, with a hussar's black mustache just below its octopus eyes, and with teeth set in its forehead. I sat up with a shriek and immediately the mustache became eyebrows and the entire face was transformed into that of my mother which I had glimpsed at first in an unwonted upside-down aspect.

And now, too, I tried to "sit up" mentally, so that the visible world might resume its everyday position—but I did not succeed. On the contrary: the closer I peered at people the more absurd their appearance looked to me. Overwhelmed with terror, I sought support in some basic idea, some better brick than the Cartesian one, with the help of which to begin the reconstruction of the simple, natural, habitual world as we know it. By that time I was resting, I believe, on the bench of a public park. I have no precise recollection of my actions. Just as a man who is having a heart attack on a sidewalk does not give a hoot for the passersby, the sun, the beauty of an ancient cathedral, and has only one concern: to breathe, so I too had but one desire: not to go mad. I am convinced that nobody ever saw the world the way I saw it during those moments, in all its terrifying nakedness and terrifying absurdity. Near me a dog was sniffing the snow. I was tortured by my efforts to recognize what "dog" might mean, and because I had been staring at it hard, it crept up to me trustingly, and I felt so nauseated that I got up from the bench and walked away. It was then that my terror reached its highest point. I gave up struggling. I was no longer a man, but a naked eye, an aimless glance moving in an absurd world. The very sight of a human face made me want to scream.

Presently I found myself again at the entrance of my hotel. Someone came up to me, pronounced my name, and thrust a folded slip of paper into my limp hand. Automatically I unfolded it, and at once my terror vanished. Everything around me became again ordinary and unobtrusive: the hotel, the changing reflections in the glass of the revolving door, the familiar face of the bellboy who had handed me the telegram. I now stood in the middle of the spacious vestibule. A man with a pipe and a checked cap brushed against me in passing and gravely apologized. I felt astonishment and an intense, unbearable but quite human pain. The telegram said she was dying.

While I traveled back, while I sat at her bedside, it never occurred to me to analyze the meaning of being and non-being and no longer was I terrified by those thoughts. The woman I loved more than anything on earth was dying. This was all I saw or felt.

She did not recognize me when my knee thudded against the side of her bed. She lay, propped up on huge pillows, under huge blankets, herself so small, with hair brushed back from the forehead revealing the narrow scar on her temple ordinarily concealed by a strand brushed low over it. She did not recognize my living presence, but by the slight smile that raised once or twice the corners of her lips, I knew that she saw me in her quiet delirium, in her dying fancy—so that there were two of me standing before her: I myself, whom she did not see, and my double, who was invisible to me. And then I remained alone: my double died with her.

Her death saved me from insanity. Plain human grief filled my life so completely that there was no room left for any other emotion. But time flows, and her image within me becomes ever more perfect, ever more lifeless. The details of the past, the live little memories, fade imperceptibly, go out one by one, or in twos and threes, the way lights go out, now here now there, in the windows of a house where people are falling asleep. And I know that my brain is doomed, that the terror I experienced once, the helpless fear of existing, will sometime overtake me again, and that then there will be no salvation.

THE ADMIRALTY
SPIRE

Although various details of the narrator's love affair match in one way or another those found in my autobiographical works, it should be firmly borne in mind that the "Katya" of the present story is an invented girl. The Admiralteyskaya Igla was written in May 1933, in Berlin, and serialized in the Poslednie Novosti, *Paris, in the issues of June 4 and 5 of that year. It was collected in* Vesna v Fialte, *Chekhov House, New York, 1956.*

YOU WILL please pardon me, dear Madam, but I am a rude and straightforward person, so I'll come right out with it: do not labor under any delusion: this is far from being a fan letter. On the contrary, as you will realize yourself in a minute, it is a rather odd little epistle that, who knows, might serve as a lesson of sorts not only for you but for other impetuous lady novelists as well. I hasten, first of all, to introduce myself, so that my visual image may show through like a watermark; this is much more honest than to encourage by silence the incorrect conclusions that the eye involuntarily draws from the calligraphy of penned lines. No, in spite of my slender handwriting and the youthful flourish of my commas, I am stout and middle-aged; true, my corpulence is not flabby, but has piquancy, zest, wasp-ishness. It is far removed, Madam, from the turndown collars of the poet Apukhtin, the fat pet of ladies. But that will do. You, as a writer, have already collected these clues to fill in the rest of me. *Bonjour, Madame.* And now let's get down to business.

The other day at a Russian library, relegated by illiterate fate to a murky Berlin alleyway, I took out three or four new items, and among them your novel *The Admiralty Spire.* Neat title—if for no other reason than that it is, isn't it, an iambic tetrameter, *admiraltéyskaya iglá*, and a famous Pushkinian line to boot. But it was the very neatness of that title that boded no good. Besides, I am generally wary of books published in the backwoods of our expatriation, such as Riga or Reval. Nevertheless, as I was saying, I did take your novel.

Ah, my dear Madam, ah, "Mr." Serge Solntsev, how easy it is to guess that the author's name is a pseudonym, that the author is not a man! Every sentence of yours buttons to the left. Your predilection for such expressions as "time passed" or "cuddled up *frileusement* in Mother's shawl," the inevitable appearance of an episodic ensign (straight from imitations of *War and Peace*) who pronounces the letter "r" as a hard "g," and, finally, footnotes with translations of French clichés, afford sufficient indication of your literary skill. But all this is only half the trouble.

Imagine the following: suppose I once took a walk through a marvelous landscape, where turbulent waters tumble and bindweed chokes the columns of desolate ruins, and then, many years later, in a stranger's house, I come across a snapshot showing me in a swaggering pose in front of what is obviously a pasteboard pillar; in the background there is the whitish smear of a daubed-in cascade, and somebody has inked a mustache on me. Where did the thing come from? Take away this horror! The dinning waters I remember were real, and, what is more, no one took a picture of me there.

Shall I interpret the parable for you? Shall I tell you that I had the same feeling, only nastier and sillier, on reading your nimble handiwork, your terrible *Spire?* As my index finger burst the uncut pages open and my eyes raced along the lines, I could only blink from the bewildering shock.

[126]

The Admiralty Spire

Do you wish to know what happened? Glad to oblige. As you lay massively in your hammock and recklessly allowed your pen to flow like a fountain (a near pun), you, Madam, wrote the story of my first love. Yes, a bewildering shock, and, as I, too, am a massive person, bewilderment is accompanied by shortness of breath. By now you and I are both puffing, for, doubtless, you are also dumbfounded by the sudden appearance of the hero that you invented. No, that was a slip—the trimmings are yours, I'll concede, and so are the stuffing and the sauce, but the game (another near pun), the game, Madam, is not yours but mine, with my buckshot in its wing. I am amazed—where and how could a lady unknown to me have kidnapped my past? Must I admit the possibility that you are acquainted with Katya—that you are close friends, even—and that she blabbed the whole business, as she whiled away summer crepuscles under the Baltic pines with you, the voracious novelist? But how did you dare, where did you find the gall not only to use Katya's tale, but, on top of that, to distort it so irreparably?

Since the day of our last meeting there has been a lapse of sixteen years—the age of a bride, an old dog, or the Soviet republic. Incidentally, let us note the first, but not the worst by far, of your innumerable and sloppy mistakes: Katya and I are not coevals. I was going on eighteen, and she on twenty. Relying on a tried and true method, you have your heroine strip before a full-length mirror whereupon you proceed to describe her loose hair, ash-blond of course, and her young curves. According to you her cornflower eyes would turn violet in pensive moments—a botanical miracle! You shaded them with the black fringe of lashes which, if I may make a contribution of my own,

[127]

seemed longer toward the outer corners, giving her eyes a very special, though illusory, slant. Katya's figure was graceful, but she cultivated a slight stoop, and would lift her shoulders as she entered a room. You make her a stately maiden with contralto tones in her voice.

Sheer torture. I had a mind to copy out your images, all of which ring false, and scathingly juxtapose my infallible observations, but the result would have been "nightmarish nonsense," as the real Katya would have said, for the Logos allotted me does not possess sufficient precision or power to get disentangled from you. On the contrary, I myself get bogged down in the sticky snares of your conventional descriptions, and have no strength left to liberate Katya from your pen. Nevertheless, like Hamlet, I will argue, and, in the end, will outargue you.

The theme of your concoction is love: a slightly decadent love with the February Revolution for backdrop, but still, love. Katya has been renamed Olga by you, and I have become Leonid. Well and good. Our first encounter, at the house of friends on Christmas Eve; our meetings at the Yusupov Skating Rink; her room, its indigo wallpaper, its mahogany furniture, and its only ornament, a porcelain ballerina with lifted leg—this is all right, this is all true. Except that you managed to give it all a taint of pretentious fabrication. As he takes his seat at the Parisiana Cinema on Nevsky Avenue, Leonid, a student of the Imperial Lyceum, puts his gloves in his three-corned hat, while a couple of pages later he is already wearing civilian clothes: he doffs his bowler, and the reader is faced by an elegant young man, with his hair parted *à l'anglaise* exactly in the middle of his small, lacquered-looking head, and a purple handkerchief drooping out of his breast pocket. I do in fact remember dressing like the film actor Max Linder, and recall the generous spurts of *Vezhetal* lotion cooling my scalp, and Monsieur Pierre taking aim with his comb and flipping my hair over with a linotype swing, and then, as he yanked off the sheet, yelling to a middle-aged, mustachioed fellow, "Boy! Bross off the 'air!" Today my memory reacts with irony to the breast-pocket handkerchief and white spats of those days, but, on the other hand, can in no way reconcile the remembered torments of adolescent shaving with your Leonid's "smooth opaque pallor." And I shall leave on your conscience his Lermontovian lusterless eyes and aristocratic profile, as it is impossible to discern much today because of an unexpected increase in fleshiness.

Good Lord, keep me from bogging down in the prose of this lady writer, whom I do not know and do not wish to know, but who has encroached with astonishing insolence on another person's past! How dare you write, "The pretty Christmas tree with its *chatoyant* lights seemed to augur to them joy jubilant"? You have extinguished the whole tree with your breath, for one adjective placed after the noun for the sake of elegance is enough to kill the best of recollections. Before the disaster, i.e., before your book, one such recollection of mine was the rippling, fragmentary light in Katya's eyes, and the cherry reflection on her cheek from the glossy little dollhouse of plasmic paper hanging on a branch as, brushing aside the bristly foliage, she stretched to pinch out the flame of a candle that had gone berserk. What do I have left of all this? Nothing—just a nauseating whiff of literary combustion.

Your version gives the impression that Katya and I inhabited a kind of exquisitely cultured beau monde. You have your parallax wrong, dear lady. That upperclass milieu—the fashionable set, if you will—to which Katya belonged, had backward tastes, to put it mildly. Chekhov was considered an "impressionist," the society rhymster Grand-Duke Constantine, a major poet, and the arch-Christian Alexander Blok a wicked Jew who wrote futuristic sonnets about dying swans and lilac liqueurs. Handwritten copies of album verse, French and English, made the rounds, and were recopied in turn, not without distortions, while the author's name imperceptibly vanished, so that those outpourings quite accidentally assumed a glamorous anonymity; and, generally speaking, it is amusing to juxtapose their meanderings with the clandestine copying of seditious jingles practiced in lower circles. A good indication of how undeservedly these male and female monologues about love were considered most modern examples of foreign lyricism is the fact that the darling among them was a piece by poor Louis Bouilhet, who wrote in the middle of last century. Reveling in the rolling cadences, Katya would declaim his alexandrines, and scold me for finding fault with a certain highly sonorous strophe in which, after having referred to his passion as a violin bow, the author compares his mistress to a guitar.

Apropos of guitars, Madam, you write that "in the evening the young people would gather and Olga would sit at a table and sing in a rich contralto." Oh well—one more death, one more victim of your sumptuous prose. Yet how I cherished the echoes of modish *tziganshchina* that inclined Katya to singing, and me to composing verse! Well do I know that this was no longer authentic Gypsy art such as that which enchanted Pushkin and, later, Apollon Grigoriev, but a barely breathing, jaded and doomed muse; everything contributed to her ruin: the gramophone, the war, and various so-called *tzigane* songs. It was for good reason that Blok, in one of his customary spells of providence, wrote down whatever words he remembered from Gypsy lyrics, as if hastening to save at least this before it was too late.

Should I tell you what those husky murmurs and plaints meant to us? Should I reveal to you the image of a distant, strange world where:

> *Pendulous willow boughs slumber*
> *Drooping low over the pond,*

Where, deep in the lilac bushes,

> *The nightingale sobs out her passion,*

and where all the senses are dominated by the memory of lost love, that wicked ruler of pseudo-Gypsy romanticism? Katya and I also would have liked to reminisce, but, since we had nothing yet to reminisce about, we would counterfeit the remoteness of time and push back into it our immediate happiness. We transformed everything we saw into monuments to our still nonexistent past by trying to look at a garden path, at the moon, at the weeping willows, with the same eyes with which *now*—when fully conscious of irreparable losses—we might have looked at that old, waterlogged raft on the pond, at that moon above the black cow shed. I even suppose that, thanks to a vague inspiration, we were preparing in advance for certain things, training ourselves to remember, imagining a distant past and practicing nostalgia, so that subsequently, when that past really existed for us, we would know how to cope with it, and not perish under its burden.

But what do you care about all this? When you describe my summer sojourn at the ancestral estate you dub "Glinskoye," you chase me into the woods and there compel me to write verse "redolent of youth and faith in life." This was all not quite so. While the others played tennis (using a single red ball and some Doherty rackets, heavy and saggy, found in the attic) or croquet on a ridiculously overgrown lawn with a dandelion in front of every hoop, Katya and I would make for the kitchen garden, and, squatting there, gorge ourselves on two species of strawberry—the bright-crimson "Victoria" (*sadovaya zemlyanika*) and the Russian hautbois (*klubnika*), purplish berries often slimed by frogs; and there was also our favorite "Ananas" variety, unripe-looking, yet wonderfully sweet. Without straightening our backs, we moved, grunting, along the furrows, and the tendons behind our knees ached, and our insides filled with a rubious weight. The hot sun bore down, and that sun, and the strawberries, and Katya's frock of tussore silk with darkening blotches under the arms, and the patina of tan on the back of her neck—all of it blended into a sense of oppressive delight; and what bliss it was, without rising, still picking berries, to clasp Katya's warm shoulder and hear her soft laughter and little grunts of greed and the crunch of her joints as she rummaged under the leaves. Forgive me if I pass directly from that orchard, floating by with the blinding gleam of its hothouses and the swaying of hairy poppies along its avenues, to the watercloset where, in the pose of Rodin's Thinker, my head still hot from the sun, I composed my verse. It was dismal in all senses of the word, that verse; it contained the trills of nightingales from *tzigane* songs and bits of Blok, and helpless echoes of Verlaine: *Souvenir, Souvenir, que me*

veux-tu? L'automne . . . —even though autumn was still
far off, and my happiness shouted with its marvelous voice
nearby, probably over there, by the bowling alley, behind
the old lilac bushes under which lay piles of kitchen refuse,
and hens walked about. In the evenings, on the veranda, the
gramophone's gaping mouth, as red as the lining of a Russian general's coat, would pour forth uncontrollable Gypsy
passion; or, to the tune of "Under a Cloud the Moon's
Hidden," a menacing voice would mimic the Kaiser: "Give
me a nib and a holder, to write ultimatums it's time." And
on the garden terrace a game of *Gorodki* (townlets) was
going on: Katya's father, his collar unbuttoned, one foot
advanced in its soft house boot, would take aim with a
cudgel as if he were firing a rifle and then hurl it with force
(but wide of the mark) at the "townlet" of skittles while
the setting sun, with the tip of its final ray, brushed across
the palisade of pine trunks, leaving on each a fiery band.
And when night finally fell, and the house was asleep,
Katya and I would look at the dark house from the park
where we kept huddled on a hard, cold, invisible bench
until our bones ached, and it all seemed to us like something
that had already once happened long ago: the outline of the
house against the pale-green sky, the sleepy movements of
the foliage, our prolonged, blind kisses.

In your elegant description, with profuse dots, of that
summer, you naturally do not forget for a minute—as we
used to forget—that since February of that year the nation
was "under the rule of the Provisional Government," and
you oblige Katya and me to follow revolutionary events
with keen concern, that is, to conduct (for dozens of
pages) political and mystical conversations that—I assure
you—we never had. In the first place, I would have been

embarrassed to speak, with the righteous pathos you lend me, of Russia's destiny and, in the second place, Katya and I were too absorbed in each other to pay much attention to the Revolution. I need but say that my most vivid impression in that respect was a mere trifle: one day, on Million Street in St. Petersburg, a truck packed with jolly rioters made a clumsy but accurate swerve so as to deliberately squash a passing cat, which remained lying there, as a perfectly flat, neatly ironed, black rag (only the tail still belonged to a cat—it stood upright, and the tip, I think, still moved). At the time this struck me with some deep occult meaning, but I have since had occasion to see a bus, in a bucolic Spanish village, flatten by exactly the same method an exactly similar cat, so I have become disenchanted with hidden meanings. You, on the other hand, have not only exaggerated my poetic talent beyond recognition, but have made me a prophet besides, for only a prophet could have talked, in the fall of 1917, about the green pulp of Lenin's deceased brain, or the "inner" emigration of intellectuals in Soviet Russia.

No, that fall and that winter we talked of other matters. I was in anguish. The most awful things were happening to our romance. You give a simple explanation: "Olga began to understand that she was sensual rather than passionate, while for Leonid it was the opposite. Their risky caresses understandably inebriated her, but deep inside there always remained a little unmelted piece"—and so on, in the same vulgar, pretentious spirit. What do you understand of our love? So far, I have deliberately avoided direct discussion of it; but now, if I were not afraid of contagion by your style, I would describe in greater detail both its fire and its underlying melancholy. Yes, there was the summer, and the foliage's omnipresent rustle, and the headlong pedaling along all of the park's winding paths, to see who would be the first to race from different directions to the *rond-point*, where the red sand was covered by the writhing serpentine tracks of our rock-hard tires, and each live, everyday detail of that final Russian summer screamed at us in desperation, "I am real! I am now!" As long as all of this sunny euphoria managed to stay on the surface, the innate sadness of our love went no further than the devotion to a nonexistent past. But when Katya and I once again found ourselves in Petersburg, and it had already snowed more than once, and the wooden paving blocks were already filmed with that yellowish layer—a mixture of snow and horse dung—without which I cannot picture a Russian city, the flaw emerged, and we were left with nothing but torment.

I can see her now, in her black sealskin coat, with a big, flat muff and gray fur-trimmed boots, walking on her slender legs, as if on stilts, along a very slippery sidewalk; or in a dark, high-necked dress, sitting on a blue divan, her face heavily powdered after much crying. As I walked to her house in the evenings and returned after midnight, I would recognize amid the granite night, under a frosty sky, dove-gray with starlight, the imperturbable and immutable landmarks of my itinerary—always those same huge Petersburg objects, lone edifices of legendary times, adorning the nocturnal wastes and half-turning away from the traveler as all beauty does: it sees you not, it is pensive, and listless, its mind is elsewhere. I would talk to myself, exhorting fate, Katya, the stars, the columns of a huge, mute, abstracted cathedral; and when a desultory exchange of fire began in the dark streets, it would occur to me casually,

and not without a sense of pleasure, that I might be picked
off by a stray bullet and die right there, reclining on dim
snow, in my elegant fur coat, my bowler askew, among
scattered white paperbacks of Gumilyov's or Mandelshtam's
new collections of verse that I had dropped and that were
barely visible against the snow. Or else, sobbing and moan-
ing as I walked, I would try to persuade myself that it was
I who had stopped loving Katya, as I hastened to gather
up all I could recall of her mendacity, her presumption, her
vacuity, the pretty patch masking a pimple, the artificial
grasseyement that would appear in her speech when she
needlessly switched to French, her invulnerable weakness
for titled poetasters, and the ill-tempered, dull expression of
her eyes when, for the hundredth time, I tried to make her
tell me with whom she had spent the previous evening.
And when it was all gathered and weighed in the balance,
I would perceive with anguish that my love, burdened as it
was with all that trash, had settled and lodged only deeper,
and that not even draft horses with iron muscles could haul
it out of the morass. And the following evening again, I
would make my way through the sailor-manned identity
checks on the street corners (documents were demanded
that allowed me access at least to the threshold of Katya's
soul, and were invalid beyond that point); I would once
again go to gaze at Katya, who, at the first pitiful word of
mine, would turn into a large, rigid doll who would lower
her convex eyelids and respond in china-doll language.
When, one memorable night, I demanded that she give me
a final, super-truthful reply, Katya simply said nothing,
and, instead, remained lying motionless on the couch, her
mirrorlike eyes reflecting the flame of the candle which on
that night of historical turbulence substituted for electric

light, and, after hearing her silence through to the end, I got up and left. Three days later, I had my valet take a note to her, in which I wrote that I would commit suicide if I could not see her just once more. So one glorious morning, with a rosy round sun and creaking snow, we met on Post Office Street; I silently kissed her hand, and for a quarter of an hour, without a single word interrupting our silence, we strolled to and fro, while nearby, on the corner of the Horse Guards Boulevard, stood smoking, with feigned nonchalance, a perfectly respectable-looking man in an astrakhan cap. As she and I silently walked to and fro, a little boy passed, pulling by its string a baized hand sled with a tattered fringe, and a drain pipe suddenly gave a rattle and disgorged a chunk of ice, while the man on the corner kept smoking; then, at precisely the same spot where we had met, I just as silently kissed her hand, which slipped back into its muff forever.

> *Farewell, my anguish and my ardor,*
> *Farewell, my dream, farewell, my pain!*
> *Along the paths of the old garden*
> *We two shall never pass again.*

Yes, yes: farewell, as the *tzigane* song has it. In spite of everything you were beautiful, impenetrably beautiful, and so adorable that I could cry, ignoring your myopic soul, and the triviality of your opinions, and a thousand minor betrayals; while I, with my overambitious verse, the heavy and hazy array of my feelings, and my breathless, stuttering speech, in spite of all my love for you, must have been contemptible and repulsive. And there is no need for me to tell you what torments I went through afterwards, how I looked and looked at the snapshot in which, with a gleam on your lip and a glint in your hair, you are looking past me. Katya, why have you made such a mess of it now?

Come, let us have a calm, heart-to-heart talk. With a lugubrious hiss the air has now been let out of the arrogant rubber fatman who, tightly inflated, clowned around at the beginning of this letter; and you, my dear, are really not a corpulent lady novelist in her novelistic hammock but the same old Katya, with Katya's calculated dash of demeanor, Katya of the narrow shoulders, a comely, discreetly made-up lady who, out of silly coquetry, has concocted a worthless book. To think that you did not even spare our parting! Leonid's letter, in which he threatens to shoot Olga, and which she discusses with her future husband; that future husband, in the role of undercover agent, standing on a street corner, ready to rush to the rescue if Leonid should draw the revolver that he is clutching in his coat pocket, as he passionately entreats Olga not to go, and keeps interrupting with his sobs her level-headed words: what a disgusting, senseless fabrication! And at the end of the book you have me join the White Army and get caught by the Reds during a reconnaissance, and, with the names of two traitresses—Russia, Olga—on my lips, die valiantly, felled by the bullet of a "Hebrew-dark" commissar. How intensely I must have loved you if I still see you as you were sixteen years ago, make agonizing efforts to free our past from its humiliating captivity, and save your image from the rack and disgrace of your own pen! I honestly do not know, though, if I am succeeding. My letter smacks strangely of those rhymed epistles that you would rattle off by heart—remember?

The sight of my handwriting may surprise you

[138]

—but I shall refrain from closing, as Apukhtin does, with the invitation:

> *The sea awaits you here, as vast as love*
> *And love, vast as the sea!*

—I shall refrain, because, in the first place, there is no sea here, and, in the second, I have not the least desire to see you. For, after your book, Katya, I am afraid of you. Truly there was no point in rejoicing and suffering as we rejoiced and suffered only to find one's past besmirched in a lady's novel. Listen—stop writing books! At least let this this flop serve as a lesson. "At least," for I have the right to wish that you will be stunned by horror upon realizing what you have perpetrated. And do you know what else I long for? Perhaps, perhaps (this is a very small and sickly "perhaps," but I grasp at it and hence do not sign this letter)—perhaps, after all, Katya, in spite of everything, a rare coincidence has occurred, and it is not you that wrote that tripe, and your equivocal but enchanting image has not been mutilated. In that case, please forgive me, colleague Solntsev.

A MATTER
OF CHANCE

Sluchaynost, *one of my earliest tales, written at the beginning of 1924, in the last afterglow of my bachelor life, was rejected by the Berlin émigré daily* Rul' *("We don't print anecdotes about cocainists," said the editor, in exactly the same tone of voice in which, thirty years later, Ross of* The New Yorker *was to say, "we don't print acrostics," when rejecting* The Vane Sisters) *and sent, with the assistance of a good friend, and a remarkable writer, Ivan Lukash, to the Rigan* Segodnya, *a more eclectic émigré organ, which published it on June 22, 1924. I would never have traced it again had it not been rediscovered by Andrew Field a few years ago.*

HE HAD a job as a waiter in the international dining car of a German fast train. His name was Aleksey Lvovich Luzhin.

He had left Russia five years before, in 1919, and since then, as he made his way from city to city, had tried a good number of trades and occupations: he had worked as a farm laborer in Turkey, a messenger in Vienna, a housepainter, a sales clerk, and so forth. Now, on either side of the diner, the meadows, the hills overgrown with heather, the pine groves flowed on and on, and the bouillon steamed and splashed in the thick cups on the tray that he nimbly carried along the narrow aisle between the window tables. He waited with masterful dispatch, forking up from the dish he carried slices of beef or ham, depositing them on the plates, and in the process rapidly dipping his close-cropped head, with its tensed forehead and black, bushy eyebrows.

The car would arrive in Berlin at five P.M., and at seven it would depart in the opposite direction, toward the French border. Luzhin lived on a kind of steel seesaw: he had time to think and reminisce only at night, in a narrow nook that smelled of fish and dirty socks. His most frequent recollections were of a house in St. Petersburg, of his study there, with those leather buttons on the curves of overstuffed furniture, and of his wife Lena, of whom he had had no news for five years. At present, he felt his life wasting away. Too-frequent sniffs of cocaine had ravaged his mind; the little sores on the inside of his nostrils were eating into the septum.

When he smiled, his large teeth would flash with an especially clean luster, and this Russian ivory smile somehow endeared him to the other two waiters—Hugo, a thickset, fair-haired Berliner who made out the checks, and quick, red-haired, sharp-nosed Max, who resembled a fox, and whose job it was to take coffee and beer to the compartments. Lately, however, Luzhin smiled less often.

During the leisure hours when the crystal-bright waves of the drug beat at him, penetrating his thoughts with their radiance and transforming the least trifle into an ethereal miracle, he painstakingly noted on a sheet of paper all the various steps he intended to take in order to trace his wife. As he scribbled, with all those sensations still blissfully taut, his jottings seemed exceedingly important and correct to him. In the morning, however, when his head ached and his shirt felt clammy and sticky, he looked with bored disgust at the jerky, blurry lines. Recently, though, another idea had begun to occupy his thoughts. He began, with the same diligence, to elaborate a plan for his own death; he would draw a kind of graph indicating the rise and fall of his sense of fear; and, finally, so as to simplify matters, he set himself a definite date—the night between the first and second of August. His interest was aroused not so much by death itself as by all the details preceding it, and he would get so involved with these details that death itself would be forgotten. But as soon as he sobered up, the picturesque setting of this or that fanciful method of self-destruction would pale, and only one thing remained clear: his life had wasted away to nothing and there was no use continuing it.

The first day of August ran its course. At six-thirty in the evening, in the vast, dimly lit buffet of the Berlin station, old Princess Maria Ukhtomski sat at a bare table, obese, all in black, with a sallow face like a eunuch's. There were few people around. The brass counterweights of the suspended lamps glimmered under the high, misty ceiling. Now and then a chair was moved back with a hollow reverberation.

Princess Ukhtomski cast a stern glance at the gilt hand of the wall clock. The hand lurched forward. A minute later it shuddered again. The old lady rose, picked up her glossly black *sac de voyage* and, leaning on her big-knobbed man's cane, shuffled toward the exit.

A porter was waiting for her at the gate. The train was backing into the station. One after another, the lugubrious, iron-colored German carriages moved past. The varnished brown teak of one sleeping car bore under the center window a sign with the inscription BERLIN-PARIS; that international car, as well as the teak-lined diner, in a window of which she glimpsed the protruding elbows and head of a carroty-haired waiter, were alone reminiscent of the severely elegant prewar Nord-Express.

The train stopped with a clang of bumpers, and a long, sibilant sigh of brakes.

The porter installed Princess Ukhtomski in a second-class compartment of a Schnellzug car—a smoking compartment as she requested. In one corner, by the window, a man in a beige suit with an insolent face and an olive complexion, was already trimming a cigar.

The old Princess settled across from him. She checked, with a slow, deliberate look, whether all her things had been placed in the overhead net. Two suitcases and a basket. All there. And the glossy *sac de voyage* in her lap. Her lips made a stern chewing movement.

A German couple lumbered into the compartment, breathing heavily.

Then, a minute before the train's departure, in came a young woman with a big painted mouth and a tight black toque that covered her forehead. She arranged her belongings and stepped out into the corridor. The man in the beige suit glanced after her. She raised the window with inexperienced jerks and leaned out to say good-bye to someone. The Princess caught the patter of Russian speech.

The train started. The young woman returned to the compartment. That smile that lingered on her face died out, and was replaced by a weary look. The brick rear walls of houses went gliding past; one of them displayed the painted advertisement of a colossal cigarette, stuffed with what looked like golden straw. The roofs, wet from a rainstorm, glistened under the rays of the low sun.

Old Princess Ukhtomski could control herself no longer. She inquired gently in Russian:

"Do you mind if I put my bag here?"

The woman gave a start and replied, "Not at all, please do."

The olive and beige man in the corner peered at her over his paper.

"Well, I'm on my way to Paris," volunteered the Princess with a slight sigh. "I have a son there. I am afraid to stay in Germany, you know."

She produced an ample handkerchief from her *sac de voyage* and firmly wiped her nose, left to right and back again.

"Yes, afraid. People say there's going to be a Communist revolution in Berlin. Have you heard anything?"

The young woman shook her head. She glanced suspiciously at the man with the paper and at the German couple.

"I don't know anything. I arrived from Russia, from Petersburg, the day before yesterday."

Princess Ukhtomski's plump sallow face expressed intense curiosity. Her diminutive eyebrows crept upward.

"You don't say!"

With her eyes fixed on the tip of her gray shoe, the woman said rapidly, in a soft voice:

"Yes, a kind-hearted person helped me to get out. I'm going to Paris too now. I have relatives there."

She started taking off her gloves. A gold wedding ring slipped off her finger. Quickly she caught it.

"I keep losing my ring. Must have grown thinner or something."

She fell silent, blinking her lashes. Through the corridor window beyond the glass compartment door the even row of telegraph wires could be seen swooping upward.

Princess Ukhtomski moved closer to her neighbor.

"Tell me," she inquired in a loud whisper. "The soviet-chiks aren't doing so well now, are they?"

A telegraph pole, black against the sunset, flew past, interrupting the smooth ascent of the wires. They dropped as a flag drops when the wind stops blowing. Then furtively they began rising again. The express was traveling swiftly between the airy walls of a spacious fire-bright evening. From somewhere in the ceilings of the compartments a slight crackling kept coming, as if rain were falling on the steel roofs. The German cars swayed violently. The international one, its interior upholstered in blue cloth, rode more smoothly and silently than the others. Three waiters were laying the tables in the diner. One of them, with close-cropped hair and beetling brows, was thinking about the little vial in his breast pocket. He kept licking his lips and sniffling. The vial contained a crystalline powder and bore the brand name Kramm. He was distributing knives and forks and inserting sealed bottles into rings on the tables, when suddenly he could stand it no longer. He flashed a flustered smile toward Max Fuchs, who was lowering the thick blinds, and darted across the unsteady connecting platform into the next car. He locked himself in the toilet. Carefully calculating the jolts of the train, he poured a small mound of the powder on his thumbnail; greedily applied it to one nostril, then to the other; inhaled; with a flip of his tongue licked the sparkling dust off his nail; blinked hard a couple of times from the rubbery bitterness, and left the toilet, boozy and buoyant, his head filling with icy delicious air. As he crossed the diaphragm on his way back into the diner, he thought: how simple it would be to die right now! He smiled. He had best wait till nightfall. It would be a pity to cut short the effect of the enchanting poison.

"Give me the reservation slips, Hugo. I'll go hand them out."

"No, let Max go. Max works faster. Here, Max."

The red-haired waiter clutched the book of coupons in

his freckled fist. He slipped like a fox between the tables and into the blue corridor of the sleeper. Five distinct harp strings swooped desperately upward alongside the windows. The sky was darkening. In the second-class compartment of a German car an old woman in black, resembling a eunuch, heard out with subdued *ochs* the account of a distant, dreary life.

"And your husband—did he stay behind?"

The young woman's eyes opened wide and she shook her head:

"No. He has been abroad for quite a time. Just happened that way. In the very beginning of the revolution he traveled south to Odessa. They were after him. I was supposed to join him there, but didn't get out in time."

"Terrible, terrible. And you have had no news of him?"

"None. I remember I decided he was dead. Started to wear my ring on the chain of my cross—I was afraid they'd take that away too. Then, in Berlin, friends told me that he was alive. Somebody had seen him. Only yesterday I put a notice in the émigré paper."

She hastily produced a folded page of the *Rul'* from her tattered silk vanity bag.

"Here, take a look."

Princess Ukhtomski put on her glasses and read:

"Elena Nikolayevna Luzhin seeks her husband Aleksey Lvovich Luzhin."

"Luzhin?" she queried, taking off her glasses. "Could it be Lev Sergeich's son? He had two boys. I don't recall their names——"

Elena smiled radiantly. "Oh, how nice. That's a surprise. Don't tell me you knew his father."

"Of course, of course," began the Princess in a complacent and kindly tone. "Lyovushka Luzhin, formerly of the Uhlans. Our estates were adjacent. He used to visit us."

"He died," interposed Elena.

"Yes, yes, I heard. May his soul rest in peace. He would always arrive with his borzoi hound. I don't remember his boys well, though. I've been abroad since 1917. The younger one had light hair, I believe. And he had a stutter."

Elena smiled again.

"No, no that was his elder brother."

"Oh, well, I got them mixed up, my dear," the Princess said comfortably. "My memory is not so good. I wouldn't even have remembered Lyovushka if you had not mentioned him yourself. But now it all comes back to me. He used to ride over for evening tea and—— Oh, let me tell you—" The Princess moved a little closer and went on, in a clear slightly lilting voice, without sadness, for she knew that happy things can only be spoken of in a happy way, without grieving because they have vanished:

"Let me tell you," she went on, "we had a set of amusing plates—with a gold rim running around and, in the very center, a mosquito so lifelike that anyone who didn't know tried to brush it off.

The compartment door opened. A red-haired waiter was handing out reservation slips for dinner. Elena took one. So did the man sitting in the corner, who for some time had been trying to catch her eye.

"I brought my own food," said the Princess. "Ham and a bun."

Max went through all the cars and trotted back to the diner. In passing, he nudged his Russian fellow worker, who was standing in the car's vestibule with a napkin under his arm. Luzhin looked after Max with glistening, anxious eyes. He felt a cool, ticklish vacuum replacing his bones and organs, as if his whole body were about to sneeze the next instant, expelling his soul. He imagined for the hundredth time how he would arrange his death. He calculated every little detail, as if he were composing a chess problem. He planned to get off at night at a certain station, walk around the motionless car and place his head against the buffer's shieldlike end when another car, that was to be coupled on, approached the waiting one. The buffers would clash. Between their meeting ends would be his bowed head. It would burst like a soap bubble and turn into iridescent air. He should get a good foothold on the crosstie and press his temple firmly against the cold metal of the bumper.

"Can't you hear me? Time to go make the dinner call."

It was now Hugo speaking. Luzhin responded with a frightened smile and did what he was told, opening for an instant the compartment doors as he went, announcing loudly and hurriedly, "First call for dinner!"

In one compartment his eye fell fleetingly on the plump, yellowish face of an old woman who was unwrapping a sandwich. He was struck by something very familiar about that face. As he hurried back through the cars, he kept thinking who she might be. It was as if he had already seen her in a dream. The sensation that his body would sneeze up his soul any instant now became more concrete— any moment now I'll remember whom that old woman resembled. But the more he strained his mind, the more irritatingly the recollection would slip away. He was morose when he returned to the diner, with his nostrils dilating and a spasm in his throat that would not let him swallow.

"Oh, the hell with her—what nonsense."

The passengers, walking unsteadily and holding onto the walls, began to move through the corridors in the direction of the diner. Reflections were already glimmering in the darkened windows, even though a yellow streak of sunset was still visible there. Elena Luzhin noticed with alarm that the man in the beige suit had waited to get up when she had. He had nasty, glassy, protuberant eyes that seemed filled with dark iodine. He walked along the passage in such a way as almost to step on her, and when a jolt threw her off balance (the cars were rocking violently) he would pointedly clear his throat. For some reason she suddenly thought he must be a spy, an informer, and she knew it was silly to think so—she was no longer in Russia, after all —yet she could not get rid of the idea.

He said something as they passed through the corridor of the sleeper. She quickened her step. She crossed the joggy connecting plates to the diner, which came after the sleeper. And here, suddenly, in the vestibule of the diner, with a kind of rough tenderness the man clutched her by the upper arm. She stifled a scream and yanked away her arm so violently that she nearly lost her footing.

The man said in German, with a foreign accent, "My precious!"

Elena made a sudden about-face. Back she went, across the connecting platform, through the sleeping car, across another platform. She felt unbearably hurt. She would rather not have dinner at all than sit facing that boorish monster. "God knows what he took me for," she reflected, "And all just because I use lipstick."

"What's the matter, my dear? Aren't you having dinner?"

Princess Ukhtomski had a ham sandwich in her hand.

"No, I don't feel like it any more. Excuse me, I'm going to take a nap."

The old woman raised her thin brows in surprise, then resumed munching.

As for Elena, she leaned her head back and pretended to sleep. Soon she did doze off. Her pale, tired face twitched occasionally. The wings of her nose shone where the powder had worn off. Princess Ukhtomski lit a cigarette that had a long cardboard mouthpiece.

A half-hour later the man returned, sat down imperturbably in his corner, and worked on his back teeth with a toothpick for a while. Then he shut his eyes, fidgeted a little, and curtained his head with a flap of his overcoat, which was hanging on a hook by the window. Another half-hour went by and the train slowed. Platform lights passed like specters alongside the fogged-up windows. The car stopped with a prolonged sigh of relief. Sounds could be heard: somebody coughing in the next compartment, footsteps running past on the station platform. The train stood for a long time, while distant nocturnal whistles called out to each other. Then it jolted and began to move.

Elena awoke. The Princess was dozing, her open mouth a black cave. The German couple was gone. The man, his face covered by his coat, slept too, his legs grotesquely spread.

Elena licked her dry lips and wearily rubbed her forehead. Suddenly she gave a start: the ring was missing from her fourth finger.

For an instant she gazed, motionless, at her naked hand. Then, with a pounding heart, she began searching hastily on the seat, on the floor. She glanced at the man's sharp knee.

"Oh, my Lord, of course—I must have dropped it on the way to the dining car when I jerked free——"

She hurried out of the compartment; arms spread, swaying this way and that, holding back her tears, she traversed one car, another. She reached the end of the sleeping car and, through the rear door, saw nothing but air, emptiness, the night sky, the dark wedge of the roadbed disappearing into the distance.

She thought she had got mixed up and gone the wrong way. With a sob, she headed back.

Next to her, by the toilet door, stood a little old woman wearing a gray apron and an armband, who resembled a night nurse. She was holding a little bucket with a brush sticking out of it.

"They uncoupled the diner," said the little old woman, and for some reason sighed. "After Cologne there will be another."

In the diner that had remained behind under the vault of a station and would continue only next morning to France, the waiters were cleaning up, folding the tablecloths. Luzhin finished, and stood in the open doorway of the car's vestibule. The station was dark and deserted. Some distance away a lamp shone like a humid star through a gray cloud of smoke. The torrent of rails glistened slightly. He could not understand why the face of the old lady with the sandwich had disturbed him so deeply. Everything else was clear, only this one blind spot remained.

Red-haired, sharp-nosed Max also came out into the vestibule. He was sweeping the floor. He noticed a glint of gold in a corner. He bent down. It was a ring. He hid it in his waistcoat pocket and gave a quick look around to see if anyone had noticed. Luzhin's back was motionless in the doorway. Max cautiously took out the ring; by the dim light he distinguished a word in script and some figures engraved on the inside. "Must be Chinese," he thought. Actually, the inscription read "1-VIII-1915. Aleksey." He returned the ring to his pocket.

Luzhin's back moved. Quietly he got off the car. He walked diagonally to the next track, with a calm, relaxed gait, as if taking a stroll.

A through train now thundered into the station. Luzhin went to the edge of the platform and hopped down. The cinders crunched under his heel.

At that instant, the locomotive came at him in one hungry bound. Max, totally unaware of what happened, watched from a distance as the lighted windows flew past in one continuous stripe.

IN MEMORY OF
L. I. SHIGAEV

Andrew Field in his bibliography of my works says he has not been able to ascertain the exact date for Pamyati L. I. Shigaeva, *written in the early nineteen-thirties in Berlin, and published probably in the* Poslednie Novosti. *I am practically sure that I wrote it in the beginning of 1934. My wife and I were sharing with her cousin, Anna Feigin, the latter's charming flat in a corner house (Number 22) of Nestorstrasse, Berlin, Grunewald (where* Invitation to a Beheading *and most of* The Gift *were composed). The rather attractive, small devils in the story belong to a subspecies described there for the first time.*

LEONID IVANOVICH SHIGAEV is dead. . . . The suspension dots, customary in Russian obituaries, must represent the footprints of words that have departed on tiptoe, in reverent single file, leaving their tracks on the marble. . . . However, I would like to violate this sepulchral silence. Please allow me to . . . Just a few fragmentary, chaotic, basically uncalled-for . . . But no matter. He and I met about eleven years ago, in a year that for me was disastrous. I was virtually perishing. Picture to yourself a young, still very young, helpless and lonely person, with a perpetually inflamed soul (it feared the least contact, it was like raw flesh) and unable to cope with the pangs of an unhappy love affair. . . . I shall take the liberty of dwelling on this point for a moment.

There was nothing exceptional about that thin, bob-haired German girl, but when I used to look at her, at her suntanned cheek, at her rich fair hair, whose shiny, golden-yellow and olive-gold strands sloped so roundly in profile from crown to nape, I felt like howling with tenderness, a tenderness that just would not fit inside me simply and comfortably, but remained wedged in the door and would not budge in or out—bulky, brittle-cornered, and of no use to anyone, least of all to that lass. In short, I discovered that once a week, at her house, she betrayed me with a respectable paterfamilias, who, incidentally, was so infernally meticulous that he would bring his own shoe trees with him. It all ended with the circuslike whump of a monstrous box on the ear with which I knocked down the traitress, who rolled up in a ball where she had collapsed, her eyes glistening at me through her spread fingers—all in all quite flattered, I think. Automatically, I searched for something to throw at her, saw the china sugar bowl I had given her for Easter, took the thing under my arm and went out, slamming the door.

A footnote: this is but one of the conceivable versions of my parting with her; I had considered many of these impossible possibilities while still in the first heat of my drunken delirium, imagining now the gross gratification of a good slap; now the firing of an old Parabellum pistol, at her and at myself, at her and at the paterfamilias, only at her, only at myself; then, finally, a glacial irony, noble sadness, silence—oh, things can go in so many ways, and I have long since forgotten how they actually went.

My landlord at the time, an athletic Berliner, suffered permanently from furunculosis: the back of his neck showed a square of disgustingly pink sticking plaster with three neat apertures—for ventilation, maybe, or, for the release of the pus. I worked in an émigré publishing house for a couple of languid-looking individuals who in reality were such cunning crooks that plain people upon observing them got spasms in the chest, as when one steps onto a cloud-piercing summit. As I began coming late ("systematically late" as they called it) and missing work, or arriving in such condition that it was necessary to send me home, our relationship became unbearable, and finally, thanks to a joint effort—with the enthusiastic collaboration of the bookkeeper and of some stranger who had come in with a manuscript—I was thrown out.

My poor, my pitiful youth! I vividly visualize the ghastly little room that I rented for five dollars a month, the ghastly flowerets of the wallpaper, the ghastly lamp hanging from its cord, with a naked bulb whose manic light glowed sometimes till morn. I was so miserable there, so indecently, luxuriously miserable, that the walls to this day must be saturated with misfortune and fever, and it is unthinkable that some happy chap could have lived there after me, whistling, humming. Ten years have elapsed, and even now I can still imagine myself then, a pale youth seated in front of the shimmery mirror, with his livid forehead and black beard, dressed only in a torn shirt, guzzling cheap booze and clinking glasses with his reflection. What times those were! Not only was I of no use to anyone in the world, but I could not even imagine a set of circumstances in which someone might care a whit about me.

By dint of prolonged, persistent, solitary drinking I drove myself to the most vulgar of visions, the most Russian of all hallucinations: I began seeing devils. I saw them every evening as soon as I emerged from my diurnal dreamery to dispel with my wretched lamp the twilight that was already engulfing us. Yes, even more clearly than I now see the perpetual tremor of my hand, I saw the precious intruders and after some time I even became accustomed to their presence, as they kept pretty much to themselves. They were smallish but rather plump, the size of an overweight toad—peaceful, limp, black-skinned, more or less warty little monsters. They crawled rather than walked, but, with all their feigned clumsiness, they proved uncapturable. I remember buying a dog whip and, as soon as enough of them had gathered on my desk, I tried to give them a good lashing, but they miraculously avoided the blow; I struck again, and one of them, the nearest, only blinked, screwing up his eyes crookedly, like a tense dog that someone wishes to threaten away from some tempting bit of ordure. The others dispersed, dragging their hind legs. But they all stealthily clustered together again while I wiped up the ink spilled on the desk and picked up a prostrate portrait. Generally speaking, their densest habitat was the vicinity of my writing table; they materialized from somewhere underneath and, in leisurely fashion, their sticky bellies crepitating and smacking against the wood, made their way up the desk legs, in a parody of climbing sailors. I tried smearing their route with Vaseline but this did not help, and only when I happened to select some particularly appetizing little rotter, intently clambering upward, and swatted him with the whip or with my shoe, only then did he fall down on the floor with a fat-toad thud; but a minute later there he was again, on his way up from a different corner, his violet tongue hanging out from the strain, and once over the top he would join his comrades. They were numerous, and at first they all seemed alike to me: dark little creatures with puffy, basically rather good-natured faces; they sat in groups of five or six on the desk, on various papers, on a volume of Pushkin, glancing at me with indifference. One of them might scratch behind his ear with his foot, the long claw making a coarse scraping sound, and then freeze motionless, forgetting his leg in midair. Another would doze, uncomfortably crowding his neighbor, who, for that matter, was not blameless either: the reciprocal inconsiderateness of amphibians, capable of growing torpid in intricate attitudes. Gradually I began distinguishing them, and I think I even gave them names depending on their resemblance to acquaintances of mine or to various animals. One could make out larger and smaller specimens (although they were all of quite portable size), some were more repulsive, others more acceptable in aspect, some had lumps or tumors, others were perfectly smooth. A few had a habit of spitting at each other. Once they brought a new boy, an albino, of a cinerous tint, with eyes like beads of red caviar; he was very sleepy and glum, and gradually crawled away. With an effort of will I would manage to vanquish the spell for a moment. It was an agonizing effort, for I had to repel and hold away a horrible iron weight, for which my entire being served as a magnet: I had but to loosen my grip, to give in ever so slightly, and the phantasma would take shape again, becoming precise, growing stereoscopic, and I would experience a deceptive sense of relief—the relief of despair, alas—when I once again yielded to the hallucination, and once again the clammy mass of thick-skinned clods sat before me on the desk, looking at me sleepily and yet somehow expectantly. I tried not only the whip, but also a famous time-honored method, on which I now find myself embarrassed to enlarge, especially since I must have used it in some wrong, very wrong way. Still, the first time it did work: a certain sacramental sign with bunched fingers, pertaining to a particular religious cult, was unhurriedly performed by me at a height of a few inches above the compact group of devils and grazed them like a red-hot iron, with a succulent hiss, both pleasant and nasty; whereupon, squirming from their burns, my rascals disparted and dropped with ripe plops to the floor. But, when I repeated

[163]

the experiment with a new gathering, the effect proved weaker and after that they stopped reacting altogether, that is, they very quickly developed a certain immunity . . . but enough about that. With a laugh—what else did I have left?—I would utter *"T'foo!"* (the only expletive, by the way, borrowed by the Russian language from the lexicon of devils; see also the German *"Teufel"*), and, without undressing, go to bed (on top of the covers, of course, as I was afraid of encountering unwanted bedfellows). Thus the days passed, if one can call them days—these were not days, but a timeless fog—and when I came to I found myself rolling on the floor, grappling with my hefty landlord among the shambles of the furniture. With a desperate lunge I freed myself and flew out of the room and thence onto the stairs, and the next thing I knew I was walking down the street, trembling, disheveled, a vile bit of alien plaster sticking to my fingers, with an aching body and a ringing head, but almost totally sober.

That was when L.I. took me under his wing. "What's the matter, old man?" (We already knew each other slightly; he had been compiling a Russian-German pocket dictionary of technical terms and used to visit the office where I worked). "Wait a minute, old man, just look at yourself." Right there on the corner (he was coming out of a delicatessen shop with his supper in his briefcase) I burst into tears, and, without a word, L.I. took me to his place, installed me on the sofa, fed me liverwurst and beef-tea, and spread over me a quilted overcoat with a worn astrakhan collar. I shivered and sobbed, and presently fell asleep.

In short, I remained in his little apartment, and lived like that for a couple of weeks, after which I rented a room next door, and we continued seeing each other daily. And yet, who would think we had anything in common? We were different in every respect! He was nearly twice my age, dependable, debonair, portly, dressed generally in a cutaway coat, cleanly and thrifty, like the majority of our orderly, elderly émigré bachelors: it was worth seeing, and especially hearing, how methodically he brushed his trousers in the morning: the sound of that brushing is now so intimately associated with him, so prominent in my recollection of him—especially the rhythm of the process, the pauses between spells of scraping, when he would stop to examine a suspicious place, scratch at it with his fingernail, or hold it up to the light. Oh, those "inexpressibles" (as he called them), that let the sky's azure shine through at the knees, his inexpressibles, inexpressibly spiritualized by that ascension!

His room was characterized by the naive neatness of poverty. He would imprint his address and telephone number on his letters with a rubber stamp (a rubber stamp!). He knew how to make *botviniya*, a cold soup of beet tops. He was capable of demonstrating for hours on end some little trinket he considered a work of genius, a curious cufflink or cigarette lighter sold to him by a smooth-talking hawker (note that L.I. himself did not smoke), or his pets, three diminutive turtles with hideous cronelike necks; one of them perished in my presence when it crashed down from a round table along the edge of which it used to keep moving, like a hurrying cripple, under the impression that it was following a straight course, leading far, far away. Another thing that I just remembered with such clarity: on the wall above his bed, which was as smooth as a prisoner's cot, hung two lithographs: a view of the Neva from the *Columna Rostrata* side and a portrait of Alexander I. He had happened to acquire them in a moment of yearning for the Empire, a nostalgia he distinguished from the yearning for one's native land.

L.I. totally lacked any sense of humor, and was totally indifferent to art, literature, and what is commonly known as nature. If the talk did happen to turn, say, to poetry, his contribution would be limited to a statement like "No, say what you will, but Lermontov is somehow closer to us than Pushkin." And when I pestered him to quote even a single line of Lermontov, he made an obvious effort to recall something out of Rubinstein's opera *The Demon*, or else answered, "Haven't reread him in a long while, 'all these are deeds of bygone days,' and, anyway, my dear Victor, just let me alone." Incidentally, he did not realize that he was quoting from Pushkin's *Ruslan and Ludmila*.

In the summer, on Sundays, he would invariably go on a trip out of town. He knew the outskirts of Berlin in astonishing detail and prided himself on his knowledge of "wonderful spots" unfamiliar to others. This was a pure, self-sufficient delight, related, perhaps, to the delights of collectors, to the orgies indulged in by amateurs of old catalogues; otherwise it was incomprehensible why he needed it all: painstakingly preparing the route, juggling various means of transportation (there by train, then back to this point by steamer, thence by bus, and this is how much it costs, and nobody, not even the Germans themselves, knows it is so cheap). But when he and I finally stood in the woods it turned out that he could not tell the difference between a bee and a bumblebee, or between alder and hazel, and perceived his surroundings quite conventionally and collectively: greenery, fine weather, the feathered tribe, little bugs. He was even offended if I, who had grown up in the country, remarked, for the sake of a bit of fun, on the differences between the flora around us and a forest in central Russia: he felt that there existed no significant difference, and that sentimental associations alone mattered.

He liked to stretch out on the grass in a shady spot, prop himself up on his right elbow, and discourse lengthily on the international situation or tell stories about his brother Peter, apparently quite a dashing fellow—ladies' man, musician, brawler—who, back in prehistoric times, drowned one summer night in the Dnepr—a very glamorous end. In dear old L.I.'s account, though, it all turned out so dull, so thorough, so well rounded out, that when, during a rest in the woods, he would suddenly ask with a kind smile: "Did I ever tell you about the time Pete took a ride on the village priest's she-goat?" I felt like crying out, "Yes, yes, you did, please spare me!"

What would I not give to hear his uninteresting yarns now, to see his absent-minded, kindly eyes, that bald pate, rosy from the heat, those graying temples. What, then, was the secret of his charm, if everything about him was so dull? Why was everybody so fond of him, why did they all cling to him? What did he do in order to be so well liked? I don't know. I don't know the answer. I only know that I felt uneasy during his morning absences when he would leave for his Institute of Social Sciences (where he spent the time poring over bound volumes of *Die Ökonomische Welt*, from which he would copy in a neat, minute hand, excerpts that in his opinion were significant and noteworthy in the utmost), or for a private lesson of Russian, which he eternally taught to an elderly couple and the elderly couple's son-in-law; his association with them led him to make many incorrect conclusions about the German way of life—on which the members of our intelligentsia (the most unobservant race in the world) consider themselves authorities. Yes, I would feel uneasy, as though I had a premonition of what has since happened to him in Prague: heart failure in the street. How happy he was, though, to get that job in Prague, how he beamed! I have an exceptionally clear recollection of the day we saw him off. Just think, a man gets the opportunity to lecture on his favorite subject! He left me a pile of old magazines (nothing grows old and dusty as fast as a Soviet magazine), his shoe trees (shoe trees were destined to pursue me) and a brand-new fountain pen (as a memento). He showed great concern for me as he left, and I know that afterwards, when our correspondence somehow wilted and ceased, and life again crashed into deep darkness—a darkness howling with thousands of voices, from which it is unlikely I will ever escape —L.I., I know, kept thinking about me, questioning people, and trying to help indirectly. He left on a beautiful summer day; tears welled persistently in the eyes of some of those seeing him off; a myopic Jewish girl with white gloves and a lorgnette brought a whole sheaf of poppies and cornflowers; L.I. inexpertly sniffed them, smiling. Did it occur to me that I might be seeing him for the last time?

Of course it did. That is exactly what occurred to me: yes, I am seeing you for the last time; this, in fact is what I always think, about everything, about everyone. My life is a perpetual good-bye to objects and people, that often do not pay the least attention to my bitter, brief, insane salutation.

BACHMANN

Bakhman *was written in Berlin, in October 1924. It was serialized in* Rul', *November 2 and 4 of that year, and included in my* Vozvrashchenie Chorba *collection of short stories, Slovo, Berlin, 1930. I am told that a pianist existed with some of my invented musician's peculiar traits. In certain other respects he is related to Luzhin, the chess player of* The Defense *(Zashchita Luzhina, 1930), G. P. Putnam's Sons, New York, 1964.*

THERE WAS a fleeting mention in the newspapers not long ago that the once famous pianist and composer Bachmann had died, forgotten by the world, in the Swiss hamlet of Marival, at the St. Angelica Home. This brought to my mind the story about a woman who loved him. It was told me by the impresario Sack. Here it is.

Mme. Perov met Bachmann some ten years before his death. In those days the golden throb of the deep and demented music he played was already being preserved on wax, as well as being heard live in the world's most famous concert halls. Well, one evening—one of those limpid-blue autumn evenings when one feels more afraid of old age than of death—Mme. Perov received a note from a friend. It read "I want to show you Bachmann. He will be at my house after the concert tonight. Do come."

I imagine with particular clarity how she put on a black, décolleté dress, flicked perfume onto her neck and shoulders, took her fan and her turquoise knobbed cane, cast a parting glance at herself in the trifold depths of a tall mirror, and sunk into a reverie that lasted all the way to her friend's house. She knew that she was plain and too thin, and that her skin was pale to the point of sickliness; yet this faded woman, with the face of a madonna that had not quite come out, was attractive thanks to the very things she was ashamed of: the pallor of her complexion, and a barely perceptible limp, which obliged her to carry a cane. Her husband, an energetic and astute businessman, was away on a trip. Sack did not know him personally.

When Mme. Perov entered the smallish, violet-lighted drawing room where her friend, a stout, noisy lady with an amethyst diadem, was fluttering heavily from guest to guest, her attention was immediately attracted by a tall man with a clean-shaven, lightly powdered face who stood leaning his elbow on the case of the piano, and entertaining with some story three ladies grouped around him. The tails of his dress coat had a substantial-looking, particularly thick silk lining, and, as he talked, he kept tossing back his dark, glossy hair, at the same time inflating the wings of his nose, which was very white and had a rather elegant hump. There was something about his entire figure benevolent, brilliant, and disagreeable.

"The acoustics were terrible!" he was saying, with a twitch of his shoulder, "and everybody in the audience had a cold. You know how it is: let one person clear his throat, and right away several others join in, and off we go." He smiled, throwing back his hair. "Like dogs at night exchanging barks in a village!"

Mme. Perov approached, leaning slightly on her cane, and said the first thing that came into her head:

"You must be tired after your concert, Mr. Bachmann?"

He bowed, very flattered.

"That's a little mistake, madame. The name is Sack. I am only the impresario of our Maestro."

All three ladies laughed. Mme. Perov lost countenance,

but laughed too. She knew about Bachmann's amazing playing only from hearsay, and had never seen a picture of him. At that moment the hostess surged toward her, embraced her, and with a mere motion of the eyes as if imparting a secret, indicated the far end of the room, whispering, "There he is—look."

Only then did she see Bachmann. He was standing a little away from the other guests. His short legs in baggy black trousers were set wide apart. He stood reading a newspaper. He held the rumpled page close up to his eyes, and moved his lips as semiliterate people do when reading. He was short, balding, with a modest lick of hair athwart the top of his head. He wore a starched turndown collar that seemed too large for him. Without taking his eyes off the paper he absent-mindedly checked the fly of his trousers with one finger, and his lips began to move with even greater concentration. He had a very funny small rounded blue chin that resembled a sea urchin.

"Don't be surprised," said Sack, "he is a barbarian in the literal sense of the word—as soon as he arrives at a party he immediately picks up something and starts reading."

Bachmann suddenly sensed that everybody was looking at him. He slowly turned his face and, raising his bushy eyebrows, smiled a wonderful, timid smile that made his entire face break out in soft little wrinkles.

The hostess hurried toward him.

"Maestro," she said, "allow me to present another of your admirers, Mme. Perov."

He thrust out a boneless, dampish hand. "Very glad, very glad indeed."

And once again he immersed himself in his newspaper.

Mme. Perov stepped away. Pinkish spots appeared on her cheekbones. The joyous to-and-fro flicker of her black fan, gleaming with jet, made the fair curls on her temples flutter. Sack told me later that on that first evening she had impressed him as an extraordinarily "temperamental" as he put it, extraordinarily high-strung, woman, despite her unpainted lips and severe hair-do.

"Those two were worth each other," he confided to me with a sigh. "As for Bachmann, he was a hopeless case, a man completely devoid of brains. And then, he drank, you know. The evening they met I had to whisk him away as on wings. He had demanded cognac all of a sudden, and he wasn't supposed to, he wasn't supposed to at all. In fact, we had begged him: 'For five days don't drink, for just five days'—he had to play those five concerts, you see. 'It's a contract, Bachmann, don't forget.' Imagine, some poet fellow in a humor magazine actually made a play on 'unsure feet' and 'forfeit'! We were literally on our last legs. And moreover, you know, he was cranky, capricious, grubby. An absolutely abnormal individual. But how he played . . ."

And, giving his thinning mane a shake, Sack rolled his eyes in silence.

As Sack and I looked through the newspaper clippings pasted in an album as heavy as a coffin, I became convinced that it was precisely then, in the days of Bachmann's first encounters with Mme. Perov, that began the real, worldwide—but, oh, how transitory!—fame of that astonishing person. When and where they became lovers, nobody knows. But after the soirée at her friend's house she began to attend all of Bachmann's concerts, no matter in what city they took place. She always sat in the first row, very straight, smooth-haired, in a black, open-necked dress. Somebody nicknamed her the Lame Madonna.

Bachmann would walk onstage rapidly, as if escaping from an enemy or simply from irksome hands. Ignoring the audience, he would hurry up to the piano, and, bending over the round stool, would begin tenderly turning the wooden disk of the seat, seeking a certain mathematically precise level. All the while he would coo, softly and earnestly, appealing to the stool in three languages. He would go on fussing thus for quite a while. English audiences were touched, French, diverted, German, annoyed. When he found the right level, Bachmann would give the stool a loving little pat and seat himself, feeling for the pedals with the soles of his ancient pumps. Then he would take out an ample, unclean handkerchief and, while meticulously wiping his hands with it, would examine the first row of seats with a mischievous, yet timid twinkle. At last he would bring his hands down softly onto the keys. Suddenly, though, a tortured little muscle would twitch under one eye; clucking his tongue, he would climb off the stool and again begin rotating its tenderly creaking disk.

Sack thinks that when she came home after hearing Bachmann for the first time, Mme. Perov sat down by the window and remained there till dawn, sighing and smiling. He insists that never before had Bachmann played with such beauty, such frenzy, and that subsequently, with every performance, his playing became still more beautiful, still more frenzied. With incomparable artistry, Bachmann would summon and resolve the voices of counterpoint, cause dissonant chords to evoke an impression of marvelous harmonies and, in his Triple Fugue, pursue the theme, gracefully, passionately toying with it, as a cat with a mouse: he would pretend he had let it escape, then, suddenly, in a flash of sly glee, bending over the keys, he would overtake it with a triumphant swoop. Then, when his engagement in that city was over, he would disappear for several days and go on a binge.

The habitués of the dubious little taverns burning venomously amid the fog of a gloomy suburb would see a small stocky man with untidy hair around a bald spot and moist eyes pink like sores, who would always choose an out-of-the-way corner, but would gladly buy a drink for anybody who happened to importune him. An old little piano tuner, long since fallen into decay, who drank with him on several occasions, decided that he followed the same trade, since Bachmann, when drunk, would drum on the table with his fingers and, in a thin, high voice, sing a very exact A. Sometimes a hardworking prostitute with high cheekbones would lead him off to her place. Sometimes he tore the violin out of the tavern fiddler's hands, stamped on it, and was thrashed in punishment. He mixed with gamblers, sailors, athletes incapacited by hernias, as well as with a guild of quiet, courteous thieves.

For nights on end Sack and Mme. Perov would look for him. It is true that Sack searched only when it was necessary to get him in shape for a concert. Sometimes they found him, and sometimes, bleary-eyed, dirty, collarless, he would appear at Mme. Perov's of his own accord; the sweet, silent lady would put him to bed, and only after two or three days would she telephone Sack to tell him that Bachmann had been found.

He combined a kind of unearthly shyness with the prankishness of a spoiled brat. He hardly talked to Mme.

Perov at all. When she remonstrated with him and tried to take him by the hands, he would break away and hit her on the fingers with shrill cries, as if the merest touch caused him impatient pain, and presently he would crawl under the blanket and sob for a long time. Sack would come and say it was time to leave for London or Rome, and take Bachmann away.

Their strange liaison lasted three years. When a more or less reanimated Bachmann was served up to the audience, Mme. Perov would invariably be sitting in the first row. On long trips they would take adjoining rooms. Mme. Perov saw her husband several times during this period. He, of course, like everybody else, knew about her rapturous and faithful passion, but he did not interfere and lived his own life.

"Bachmann made her existence a torment," Sack kept repeating. "It is incomprehensible how she could have loved him. The mystery of the female heart! Once, when they were at somebody's house together, I saw the Maestro with my own eyes suddenly begin snapping his teeth at her, like a monkey, and you know why? Because she wanted to straighten his tie. But in those days there was genius in his playing. To that period belongs his *Symphony in D Minor* and several complex fugues. No one saw him writing them. The most interesting is the so-called "Golden Fugue." Have you heard it? Its thematic development is totally original. But I was telling you about his whims and his growing lunacy. Well, here's how it was. Three years passed, and then, one night in Munich, where he was performing . . ."

And as Sack neared the end of his story, he narrowed his eyes more sadly and more impressively.

It seems that the night of his arrival in Munich Bachmann escaped from the hotel where he had stopped as usual
with Mme. Perov. Three days remained before the concert, and therefore Sack was in a state of hysterical alarm.
Bachmann could not be found. It was late autumn, with a
lot of rain. Mme. Perov caught cold and took to her bed.
Sack, with two detectives, continued to check the bars.

On the day of the concert the police telephoned to say
that Bachmann had been located. They had picked him up
in the street during the night and he had had an excellent
bit of sleep at the station. Without a word Sack drove
him from the police station to the theater, consigned him
like an object to his assistants, and went to the hotel to
get Bachmann's tailcoat. He told Mme. Perov through the
door what had happened. Then he returned to the theater.

Bachmann, his black felt hat pushed down onto his
brows, was sitting in his dressing room, sadly tapping the
table with one finger. People fussed and whispered around
him. An hour later the audience began taking their places
in the huge hall. The white, brightly lit stage, adorned by
sculptured organ pipes on either side, the gleaming black
piano, with upraised wing, and the humble mushroom of
its stool—all awaited in solemn idleness a man with moist,
soft hands who would soon fill with a hurricane of sound
the piano, the stage, and the enormous hall, where, like
pale worms, women's shoulders and men's bald pates
moved and glistened.

And now Bachmann has trotted onstage. Paying no
attention to the thunder of welcome that rose like a compact cone and fell apart in scattered, dying claps, he began
rotating the disk of the stool, cooing avidly and, having
patted it, sat down at the piano. Wiping his hands, he

glanced toward the first row with his timid smile. Abruptly his smile vanished and Bachmann grimaced. The handkerchief fell to the floor. His attentive gaze slid once again across the faces—and stumbled, as it were, upon reaching the empty seat in the center. Bachmann slammed down the lid, got up, walked out to the very edge of the stage and, rolling his eyes and raising his bent arms like a ballerina, executed two or three ridiculous *pas*. The audience froze. From the back seats came a burst of laughter. Bachmann stopped, said something that nobody could hear, and then, with a sweeping, archlike motion, showed the whole house a fico.

"It happened so suddenly," went Sack's account. "that I could not get there in time to help. I bumped into him when, after the fig—instead of the fugue—he was leaving the stage. I asked him, 'Bachmann, where are you going?' He uttered an obscenity and disappeared into the greenroom."

Then Sack himself walked out on the stage, to a storm of wrath and mirth. He raised his hand, managed to obtain silence, and gave his firm promise that the concert would take place. Upon entering the greenroom he found Bachmann sitting there as though nothing had happened, his lips moving as he read the printed program.

Sack glanced at those present, and, raising a brow meaningfully, rushed to the telephone and called Mme. Perov. For a long time he could get no answer; at last something clicked and he heard her feeble voice.

"Come here this instant," jabbered Sack, striking the telephone book with the side of his hand. "Bachmann won't play without you. It's a terrible scandal! The audience is beginning to ——What?—What's that?— Yes, yes, I keep telling you he refuses. Hello? Oh, damn!— I've been cut off ..."

Mme. Perov was worse. The doctor, who had visited her twice that day, had looked with dismay at the mercury that had climbed so high along the red ladder in its glass tube. As she hung up—the telephone was by the bed—she probably smiled happily. Tremulous and un-steady on her feet, she started to dress. An unbearable pain kept stabbing her in the chest, but happiness called to her through the haze and hum of the fever. I imagine for some reason that when she started pulling on her stockings, the silk kept catching on the toenails of her icy feet. She arranged her hair as best she could, wrapped herself in a brown fur coat, and went out, cane in hand. She told the doorman to call a taxi. The black pavement glistened. The handle of the car door was wet and ice-cold. All the way during the ride that vague, happy smile must have remained on her lips, and the sound of the motor and the hiss of the tires blended with the hot humming in her temples. When she reached the theater, she saw crowds of people opening angry umbrellas as they tumbled out into the street. She was almost knocked off her feet, but managed to squeeze through. In the greenroom Sack was pacing back and forth, clutching now at his left cheek, now at his right.

"I was in an utter rage!" he told me. "While I was struggling with the telephone, the Maestro escaped. He said he was going to the toilet, and slipped away. When Mme. Perov arrived I pounced on her—why hadn't she been sitting in the theater? You understand, I absolutely did not take into account the fact that she was ill. She asked me, 'So he's back at the hotel now? So we passed each

other on the way?' And I was in a furious state, shouting,
'The hell with hotels—he's in some bar! Some bar! Some
bar!' Then I gave up and rushed off. Had to rescue the
ticket seller."

And Mme. Perov, trembling and smiling, went to search
for Bachmann. She knew approximately where to look for
him, and it was thither, to that dark, dreadful quarter that
an astonished driver took her. When she reached the street
where, according to Sack, Bachmann had been found the
day before, she let the taxi go and, leaning on her cane,
began walking along the uneven sidewalk, under the slant-
ing streams of black rain. She entered all the bars one by
one. Bursts of raucous music deafened her and men looked
her over insolently. She would glance around the smoky,
spinning, motley tavern and go back out into the lashing
night. Soon it began to seem to her that she was continuously entering one and the same bar, and an agonizing
weakness descended upon her shoulders. She walked, limp-
ing and emitting barely audible moans, holding tightly the
turquoise knob of her cane in her cold hand. A policeman
who had been watching her for some time approached with
a slow, professional step and asked for her address, then
firmly and gently led her over to a horse cab on night
duty. In the creaking, evil-smelling murk of the cab she
lost consciousness and, when she came to, the door was
open and the driver, in a shiny oilskin cape, was giving
her little pokes in the shoulder with the butt of his whip.
Upon finding herself in the warm corridor of the hotel,
she was overcome by a feeling of complete indifference to
everything. She pushed open the door of her room and
went in. Bachmann was sitting on her bed, barefoot and in
a nightshirt, with a plaid blanket humped over his shoul-

ders. He was drumming with two fingers on the marble top of the night table, while using his other hand to make dots on a sheet of music paper with an indelible pencil. So absorbed was he that he did not notice the door open. She uttered a soft, moanlike "ach." Bachmann gave a start. The blanket started to slide off his shoulders.

I think this was the only happy night in Mme. Perov's life. I think that these two, the deranged musician and the dying woman, that night found words the greatest poets never dreamed of. When the indignant Sack arrived at the hotel the next morning, Bachmann sat there with an ecstatic, silent smile, contemplating Mme. Perov, who was lying across the wide bed, unconscious under the plaid blanket. Nobody could know what Bachmann was thinking as he looked at the burning face of his mistress and listened to her spasmodic breathing; probably he interpreted in his own fashion the agitation of her body, the flutter and fire of a fatal illness, not the least idea of which entered his head. Sack called the doctor. At first Bachmann looked at them distrustfully, with a timid smile; then he clutched at the doctor's shoulder, ran back, struck himself on the forehead, and began tossing to and fro and gnashing his teeth. She died the same day, without regaining consciousness. The expression of happiness never left her face. On the night table Sack found a crumpled sheet of music paper, but no one was able to decipher the violet dots of music scattered over it.

"I took him away immediately," Sack went on. "I was afraid of what would happen when the husband arrived, you can understand. Poor Bachmann was as limp as a rag doll and kept plugging his ears with his fingers. He would cry out as though someone were tickling him, 'Stop those sounds! Enough, enough music!' I don't really know what gave him such a shock: between you and me, he never loved that unfortunate woman. In any case, she was his undoing. After the funeral Bachmann disappeared without leaving a trace. You can still find his name in the advertisements of player-piano firms, but, generally speaking, he has been forgotten. It was only six years later that Fate brought us together again. For an instant only. I was waiting for a train at a small station in Switzerland. It was a glorious evening, I recall. I was not alone. Yes, a woman —but that's a different libretto. And then, what do you know, I see a small crowd gathered around a short man in a shabby black coat and black hat. He was thrusting a coin into a music box, and sobbing incontrollably. He would put in a coin, listen to the tinny melody, and sob. Then the roll or something broke down. The coin jammed. He began shaking the box, wept louder, gave up, and went away. I recognized him immediately, but, you understand, I was not alone, I was with a lady, and there were people around, sort of gaping. It would have been awkward to go up to him and say *Wie geht's dir*, Bachmann?"

PERFECTION

Sovershenstvo *was written in Berlin, in June 1932. It appeared in the Paris daily* Poslednie Novosti *(July 3, 1932) and was included in my collection* Soglyadatay, *Paris, 1938. Although I did tutor boys in my years of expatriation, I disclaim any other resemblance between myself and Ivanov.*

"NOW THEN, here we have two lines," he would say to David in a cheery, almost rapturous voice as if to have two lines were a rare fortune, something one could be proud of. David was gentle but dullish. Watching David's ears evolve a red glow, Ivanov foresaw he would often appear in David's dreams, thirty or forty years hence: human dreams do not easily forget old grudges.

Fair-haired and thin, wearing a yellow sleeveless jersey held close by a leather belt, with scarred naked knees and a wristwatch whose crystal was protected by a prison-window grating, David sat at the table in a most uncomfortable position, and kept tapping his teeth with the blunt end of his fountain pen. He was doing badly at school, and it had become necessary to engage a private tutor.

"Let us now turn to the second line," Ivanov continued with the same studied cheeriness. He had taken his degree in geography but his special knowledge could not be put to any use: dead riches, a highborn pauper's magnificent manor. How beautiful, for instance, are ancient charts! Viatic maps of the Romans, elongated, ornate, with snakelike marginal stripes representing canal-shaped seas; or those drawn in ancient Alexandria, with England

[187]

and Ireland looking like two little sausages; or again, maps of medieval Christendom, crimson-and-grass-colored, with the paradisian Orient at the top and Jerusalem—the world's golden navel—in the center. Accounts of marvelous pilgrimages: that traveling monk comparing the Jordan to a little river in his native Chernigov, that envoy of the Tsar reaching a country where people strolled under yellow parasols, that merchant from Tver picking his way through a dense "*zhengel*," his Russian for "jungle," full of monkeys, to a torrid land ruled by a naked prince. The islet of the known universe keeps growing: new hesitant contours emerge from the fabulous mists, slowly the globe disrobes—and lo, out of the remoteness beyond the seas, looms South America's shoulder and from their four corners blow fat-cheeked winds, one of them wearing spectacles.

But let us forget the maps. Ivanov had many other joys and eccentricities. He was lanky, swarthy, none too young, with a permanent shadow cast on his face by a black beard that had once been permitted to grow for a long time, and had then been shaven off (at a barbershop in Serbia, his first stage of expatriation): the slightest indulgence made that shadow revive and begin to bristle. Throughout a dozen years of émigré life, mostly in Berlin, he had remained faithful to starched collars and cuffs; his deteriorating shirts had an outdated tongue in front to be buttoned to the top of his long underpants. Of late he had been obliged to wear constantly his old formal black suit with braid piping along the lapels (all his other clothes having rotted away); and occasionally, on an overcast day, in a forbearing light, it seemed to him that he was dressed with sober good taste. Some sort of flannel entrails were trying to escape from his necktie, and he was forced to trim off parts of them, but could not bring himself to excise them altogether.

He would set out for his lesson with David at around three in the afternoon, with a somewhat unhinged, bouncing gait, his head held high. He would inhale avidly the young air of the early summer, rolling his large Adam's apple, which in the course of the morning had already fledged. On one occasion a youth in leather leggings attracted Ivanov's absent gaze from the opposite sidewalk by means of a soft whistle, and, throwing up his own chin, kept it up for a distance of a few steps: thou shouldst correct thy fellow man's oddities. Ivanov, however, misinterpreted that didactic mimicry and, assuming that something was being pointed out to him overhead, looked trustingly even higher than was his wont—and, indeed, three lovely cloudlets, holding each other by the hand, were drifting diagonally across the sky; the third one fell slowly behind, and its outline, and the outline of the friendly hand still stretched out to it, slowly lost their graceful significance.

During those first warm days everything seemed beautiful and touching: the leggy little girls playing hopscotch on the sidewalk, the old men on the benches, the green confetti that sumptuous lindens scattered every time the air stretched its invisible limbs. He felt lonesome and stifled in black. He would take off his hat and stand still for a moment looking around. Sometimes, as he looked at a chimneysweep (that indifferent carrier of other people's luck, whom women in passing touched with superstitious fingers), or at an airplane overtaking a cloud, Ivanov daydreamed about the many things that he would never get to know closer, about professions that he would never practice, about a parachute, opening like a colossal corolla, or the fleeting, speckled world of automobile racers, about various images of happiness, about the pleasures of very rich people amidst very picturesque natural surroundings. His thought fluttered and walked up and down the glass pane which for as long as he lived would prevent him from having direct contact with the world. He had a passionate desire to experience everything, to attain and touch everything, to let the dappled voices, the bird calls, filter through his being and to enter for a moment into a passerby's soul as one enters the cool shade of a tree. His mind would be preoccupied with unsolvable problems: How and where do chimneysweeps wash after work? Has anything changed about that forest road in Russia that a moment ago he had recalled so vividly?

When, at last, late as usual, he went up in the elevator, he would have a sensation of slowly growing, stretching upward, and, after his head had reached the sixth floor, of pulling up his legs like a swimmer. Then, having reverted to normal length, he would enter David's bright room.

During lessons David liked to fiddle with things but otherwise remained fairly attentive. He had been raised abroad and spoke Russian with difficulty and boredom, and, when faced with the necessity of expressing something important, or when talking to his mother, the Russian wife of a Berlin businessman, would immediately switch to German. Ivanov, whose knowledge of the local language was poor, expounded mathematics in Russian, while the textbook was of course, in German, and this produced a certain amount of confusion. As he watched the boy's ears, edged with fair down, he tried to imagine the degree of tedium and detestation he must arouse in

David, and this distressed him. He saw himself from the outside—a blotchy complexion, a *feu du rasoir* rash, a shiny black jacket, stains on its sleeve cuffs—and caught his own falsely animated tone, the throat-clearing noises he made, and even that sound which could not reach David—the blundering but dutiful beat of his long-ailing heart. The lesson came to an end, the boy would hurry to show him something, such as an automobile catalogue, or a camera, or a cute little screw found in the street—and then Ivanov did his best to give proof of intelligent participation—but, alas, he never had been on intimate terms with the secret fraternity of man-made things that goes under the name technology, and this or that inexact observation of his would make David fix him with puzzled pale-gray eyes and quickly take back the object which seemed to be whimpering in Ivanov's hands.

And yet David was not untender. His indifference to the unusual could be explained—for I, too, reflected Ivanov, must have appeared to be a stolid and dryish lad, I who never shared with anyone my loves, my fancies and fears. All that my childhood expressed was an excited little monologue addressed to itself. One might construct the following syllogism: a child is the most perfect type of humanity; David is a child; David is perfect. With such adorable eyes as he has, a boy cannot possibly keep thinking only about the prices of various mechanical gadgets or about how to save enough trading stamps to obtain fifty pfennigs' worth of free merchandise at the store. He must be saving up something else, too: bright childish impressions whose paint remains on the fingertips of the mind. He keeps silent about it just as I kept silent. But if several decades later—say, in 1970 (how they resemble telephone numbers, those distant years!) he will happen to see again that picture now hanging above his bed— Bonzo devouring a tennis ball—what a jolt he will feel, what light, what amazement at his own existence. Ivanov was not entirely wrong, David's eyes, indeed, were not devoid of a certain dreaminess; but it was the dreaminess of concealed mischief.

Enters David's mother. She has yellow hair and a high-strung temperament. The day before she was studying Spanish; today she subsists on orange juice. "I would like to speak to you. Stay seated, please. Go away, David. The lesson is over? David, go. This is what I want to say. His vacation is coming soon. It would be appropriate to take him to the seaside. Regrettably, I shan't be able to go myself. Would you be willing to take him along? I trust you, and he listens to you. Above all, I want him to speak Russian more often. Actually he's nothing but a little *Sportsmann* as are all modern kids. Well, how do you look at it?"

With doubt. But Ivanov did not voice his doubt. He had last seen the sea in 1912, eighteen years ago when he was a university student. The resort was Hungerburg in the province of Estland. Pines, sand, silvery-pale water far away—oh, how long it took one to reach it, and then how long it took it to reach up to one's knees! It would be the same Baltic Sea, but a different shore. However, the last time I went swimming was not at Hungerburg but in the river Luga. Muzhiks came running out of the water, frog-legged, hands crossed over their private parts: *pudor agrestis*. Their teeth chattered as they pulled on their shirts over their wet bodies. Nice to go bathing in the river toward evening, especially under a warm rain that makes silent circles, each spreading and encroaching upon the next, all over the water. But I like to feel underfoot the presence of the bottom. How hard to put on again one's socks and shoes without muddying the soles of one's feet! Water in one's ear: keep hopping on one foot until it spills out like a tickly tear.

The day of departure soon came. "You will be frightfully hot in those clothes," remarked David's mother by way of farewell as she glanced at Ivanov's black suit (worn in mourning for his other defunct things). The train was crowded, and his new, soft collar (a slight compromise, a summer treat) turned gradually into a tight clammy compress. Happy David, his hair neatly trimmed, with one small central tuft playing in the wind, his open-necked shirt aflutter, stood, at the corridor window, peering out, and on curves the semicircles of the front cars would become visible, with the heads of passengers who leant on the lowered frames. Then the train, its bell ringing, its elbows working ever so rapidly, straightened out again to enter a beech forest.

The house was located at the rear of the little seaside town, a plain two-storied house with red-currant shrubs in the yard, which a fence separated from the dusty road. A tawny-bearded fisherman sat on a log, slitting his eyes in the low sun as he tarred his net. His wife led them upstairs. Terra-cotta floors, dwarf furniture. On the wall, a fair-sized fragment of an airplane propeller: "My husband used to work at the airport." Ivanov unpacked his scanty linen, his razor, and a dilapidated volume of Pushkin's works in the Panafidin edition. David freed from its net a varicolored ball that went jumping about and from sheer exuberance only just missed knocking a horned shell off its shelf. The landlady brought tea and some flounder. David was in a hurry. He could not wait to get a look at the sea. The sun had already begun to set.

When they came down to the beach after a fifteen-minute walk, Ivanov instantly became conscious of an acute discomfort in his chest, a sudden tightness followed by a sudden void, and out on the smooth, smoke-blue sea a small boat looked black and appallingly alone. Its imprint began to appear on whatever he looked at, then dissolved in the air. Because now the dust of twilight dimmed everything around, it seemed to him that his eyesight was dulled, while his legs felt strangely weakened by the squeaky touch of the sand. From somewhere came the playing of an orchestra, and its every sound, muted by distance, seemed to be corked up; breathing was difficult. David chose a spot on the beach and ordered a wicker cabana for next day. The way back was uphill; Ivanov's heart now drifted away, then hurried back to perform anyhow what was expected of it, only to escape again, and through all this pain and anxiety the nettles along the fences smelled of Hungerburg.

David's white pyjama. For reasons of economy Ivanov slept naked. At first the earthen cold of the clean sheets made him feel even worse, but then repose brought relief. The moon groped its way to the washstand, selected there one facet of a tumbler, and started to crawl up the wall. On that and on the following nights, Ivanov thought vaguely of several matters at once, imagining among other things that the boy who slept in the bed next to his was his own son. Ten years before, in Serbia, the only woman he had ever loved—another man's wife—had become pregnant by him. She suffered a miscarriage and died the next night, deliring and praying. He would have had a son, a little fellow about David's age. When in the morning David prepared to pull on his swimming trunks, Ivanov was touched by the way his *café-au-lait* tan (already acquired on a Berlin lakeside) abruptly gave way to a childish whiteness below the waist. He was about to forbid the boy to go from house to beach with nothing on but those trunks, and was a little taken aback, and did not immediately give in, when David began to argue, with the whining intonations of German astonishment, that he had done so at another resort and that everyone did it. As to Ivanov, he languished on the beach in the sorrowful image of a city dweller. The sun, the sparkling blue, made him seasick. A hot tingling ran over the top of his head under his fedora, he felt as if he were being roasted alive, but he would not even dispense with his jacket, not only because as is the case with many Russians, it would embarrass him to "appear in his braces in the presence of ladies," but also because his shirt was too badly frayed. On the third day he suddenly gathered up his courage and, glancing furtively around from under his brows, took off his shoes. He settled at the bottom of a crater dug by David, with a newspaper sheet spread under his elbow, and listened to the tight snapping of the gaudy flags, or else peered over the sandy brink with a kind of tender envy, at a thousand brown corpses felled in various attitudes by the sun; one girl was especially magnificent, as if cast in metal, tanned to the point of blackness, with amazingly light eyes and with fingernails as pale as a monkey's. Looking at her he tried to imagine what it felt like to be so sun-baked.

On obtaining permission for a dip, David would noisily swim off while Ivanov walked to the edge of the surf to watch his charge and to jump back whenever a wave spreading farther than its predecessors threatened to douse his trousers. He recalled a fellow student in Russia, a close friend of his, who had the knack of pitching pebbles so as to have them glance off the water's surface two, three, four times, but when he tried to demonstrate it to David, the projectile pierced the surface with a loud plop, and David laughed, and made a nice flat stone perform not four but at least six skips.

A few days later, during a spell of absentmindedness (his eyes had strayed, and it was too late when he caught up with them), Ivanov read a postcard that David had begun writing to his mother and had left lying on the window ledge. David wrote that his tutor was probably ill for he never went swimming. That very day Ivanov took extraordinary measures: He acquired a black bathing suit and, on reaching the beach, hid in the cabana, undressed gingerly, and pulled on the cheap shop-smelling stockinet garment. He had a moment of melancholy embarrassment when, pale-skinned and hairy-legged, he emerged into the sunlight. David, however, looked at him with approval. "Well!" exclaimed Ivanov with devil-may-care jauntiness, "here we go!" He went in up to his knees, splashed some water on his head, then walked on with outspread arms, and the higher the water rose, the deadlier became the spasm that contracted his heart. At last, closing his ears with his thumbs, and covering his eyes with the rest of his fingers, he immersed himself in a crouching position. The stabbing chill compelled him to get promptly out of the water. He lay down on the sand, shivering and filled to the brim of his being with ghastly, unresolvable anguish.

Perfection

After a while the sun warmed him, he revived, but from then on forswore sea bathing. He felt too lazy to dress; when he closed his eyes tightly, optical spots glided against a red background, Martian canals kept intersecting, and, the moment he parted his lids, the wet silver of the sun started to palpitate between his lashes.

The inevitable took place. By evening, all those parts of his body that had been exposed turned into a symmetrical archipelago of fiery pain. "Today, instead of going to the beach, we shall take a walk in the woods," he said to the boy on the morrow. "*Ach, nein,*" wailed David. "Too much sun is bad for the health," said Ivanov. "Oh, please!" insisted David in great dismay. But Ivanov stood his ground.

The forest was dense. Geometrid moths, matching the bark in coloration, flew off the tree trunks. Silent David walked reluctantly. "We should cherish the woods," Ivanov said in an attempt to divert his pupil. "It was the first habitat of man. One fine day man left the jungle of primitive intimations for the sunlit glade of reason. Those bilberries appear to be ripe, you have my permission to taste them. Why do you sulk? Try to understand: one should vary one's pleasures. And one should not over-indulge in sea bathing. How often it happens that a careless bather dies of sun stroke or heart failure!"

Ivanov rubbed his unbearably burning and itching back against a tree trunk and continued pensively: "While admiring nature at a given locality, I cannot help thinking of countries that I shall never see. Try to imagine, David, that this is not Pomerania but a Malayan forest. Look about you: you'll presently see the rarest of birds fly past,

Prince Albert's paradise bird, whose head is adorned with a pair of long plumes consisting of blue oriflammes."

"*Ach, quatsch,*" responded David dejectedly.

"In Russian you ought to say '*erundá.*' Of course, it's nonsense, we are not in the mountains of New Guinea. But the point is that with a bit of imagination—if, God forbid, you were some day to go blind or be imprisoned, or were merely forced to perform, in appalling poverty, some hopeless, distasteful task, you might remember this walk we are taking today in an ordinary forest as if it had been—how shall I say?—fairytale ecstasy."

At sundown dark-pink clouds fluffed out above the sea. With the dulling of the sky they seemed to rust, and a fisherman said it would rain tomorrow, but the morning turned out to be marvelous and David kept urging his tutor to hurry, but Ivanov was not feeling well; he longed to stay in bed and think of remote and vague semievents illumined by memory on only one side, of some pleasant smoke-gray things that might have happened once upon a time, or drifted past quite close to him in life's field of vision, or else had appeared to him in a recent dream. But it was impossible to concentrate on them, they all somehow slipped away to one side, half-turning to him with a kind of friendly and mysterious slyness but gliding away relentlessly, as do those transparent little knots that swim diagonally in the vitreous humor of the eye. Alas, he had to get up, to pull on his socks, so full of holes that they resembled lace mittens. Before leaving the house he put on David's dark-yellow sunglasses—and the sun swooned amidst a sky dying a turquoise death, and the morning light upon the porch steps acquired a sunset tinge. David, his naked back amber colored, ran ahead, and when Ivanov called to him, he shrugged his shoulders in irritation. "Do not run away," Ivanov said wearily. His horizon was narrowed by the glasses, he was afraid of a sudden automobile.

The street sloped sleepily toward the sea. Little by little his eyes became used to the glasses, and he ceased to wonder at the sunny day's khaki uniform. At the turn of the street he suddenly half-remembered something—something extraordinarily comforting and strange—but it immediately dissolved, and the turbulent sea air constricted his chest. The dusky flags flapped excitedly, pointing all in the same direction, though nothing was happening there yet. Here is the sand, here is the dull splash of the sea. His ears felt plugged up, and when he inhaled through the nose a rumble started in his head, and something bumped into a membranous dead end. "I've lived neither very long nor very well," reflected Ivanov. "Still it would be a shame to complain; this alien world is beautiful, and I would feel happy right now if only I could recall that wonderful, wonderful—what? What was it?"

He lowered himself onto the sand. David began busily repairing with a spade the sand wall where it had crumbled slightly. "Is it hot or cool today?" asked Ivanov. "Somehow I cannot decide." Presently David threw down the spade and said, "I'll go for a swim." "Sit still for a moment," said Ivanov. "I must gather my thoughts. The sea will not run away." "*Please* let me go!" pleaded David.

Ivanov raised himself on one elbow and surveyed the waves. They were large and humpbacked; nobody was bathing at that spot; only much further to the left a dozen orange-capped heads bobbed and were carried off to one side in unison. "Those waves," said Ivanov with a sigh, and then added: "You may paddle a little, but don't go beyond a *sazhen*. A *sazhen* equals about two meters."

He sank his head, propping one cheek, grieving, computing indefinite measures of life, of pity, of happiness. His shoes were already full of sand, he took them off with slow hands, then was again lost in thought, and again those evasive little knots began to swim across his field of vision—and how he longed, how he longed to recall—— A sudden scream. Ivanov stood up.

Amidst yellow-blue waves, far from the shore, flitted David's face, and his open mouth was like a dark hole. He emitted a spluttering yell, and vanished. A hand appeared for a moment and vanished too. Ivanov threw off his jacket. "I'm coming," he shouted. "I'm coming. Hold on!" He splashed through the water, lost his footing, his ice-cold trousers stuck to his shins. It seemed to him that David's head came up again for an instant. Then a wave surged, knocking off Ivanov's hat, blinding him; he wanted to take off his glasses, but his agitation, the cold, the numbing weakness, prevented him from doing so. He realized that in its retreat the wave had dragged him a long way from the shore. He started to swim trying to catch sight of David. He felt enclosed in a tight painfully cold sack, his heart was straining unbearably. All at once a rapid something passed through him, a flash of fingers rippling over piano keys— and *this* was the very thing he had been trying to recall throughout the morning. He came out on a stretch of sand. Sand, sea, and air were of an odd, faded, opaque tint, and everything was perfectly still. Vaguely he reflected that twilight must have come, and that David had perished a long time ago, and he felt what he knew from earthly life—the poignant heat of tears. Trembling and bending toward the ashen sand, he wrapped himself tighter in the black cloak with the snake-shaped brass fastening that he had seen on a student friend, a long, long time ago, on an autumn day—and he felt so sorry for David's mother, and wondered what would he tell her. It is not my fault, I did all I could to save him, but I am a poor swimmer, and I have a bad heart, and he drowned. But there was something amiss about these thoughts, and when he looked around once more and saw himself in the desolate mist all alone with no David beside him, he understood that if David was not with him, David was not dead.

Only then were the clouded glasses removed. The dull mist immediately broke, blossomed with marvelous colors, all kinds of sounds burst forth—the rote of the sea, the clapping of the wind, human cries—and there was David standing, up to his ankles in bright water, not knowing what to do, shaking with fear, not daring to explain that he had not been drowning, that he had struggled in jest—and farther out people were diving, groping through the water, then looking at each other with bulging eyes, and diving anew, and returning empty-handed, while others shouted to them from the shore, advising them to search a little to the left; and a fellow with a Red Cross armband was running along the beach, and three men in sweaters were pushing into the water a boat grinding against the shingle; and a bewildered David was being led away by a fat woman in a pince-nez, the wife of a veterinary, who had been expected to arrive on Friday but had had to postpone his vacation, and the Baltic Sea sparkled from end to end, and, in the thinned-out forest, across a green country road, there lay, still breathing, freshly cut aspens; and a youth, smeared with soot, gradually turned white as he washed under the kitchen tap, and black parakeets flew above the eternal snows of the New Zealand mountains; and a fisherman, squinting in the sun, was solemnly predicting that not until the ninth day would the waves surrender the corpse.

VASILIY SHISHKOV

To relieve the dreariness of life in Paris at the end of 1939 (about six months later I was to migrate to America) I decided one day to play an innocent joke on the most famous of émigré critics, George Adamovich (who used to condemn my stuff as regularly as I did the verse of his disciples) by publishing in one of the two leading magazines a poem signed with a new pen name, so as to see what he would say, about that freshly emerged author, in the weekly literary column he contributed to the Paris émigré daily Poslednie Novosti. *Here is the poem, as translated by me in 1970* (Poems and Problems, McGraw-Hill, New York):

THE POETS

From room to hallway a candle passes
and is extinguished. Its imprint swims in one's eyes,
until, among the blue-black branches,
a starless night its contours finds.

It is time, we are going away: still youthful,
with a list of dreams not yet dreamt,
with the last, hardly visible radiance of Russia
on the phosphorent rhymes of our last verse.

[204]

Vasiliy Shishkov

And yet we did know—didn't we?—inspiration,
we would live, it seemed, and our books would grow
but the kithless muses at last have destroyed us,
and it is time now for us to go.

And this not because we're afraid of offending
with our freedom good people; simply, it's time
for us to depart—and besides we prefer not
to see what lies hidden from other eyes;

not to see all this world's enchantment and torment,
the casement that catches a sunbeam afar,
humble somnambulists in soldier's uniform,
the lofty sky, the attentive clouds;

the beauty, the look of reproach; the young children
who play hide-and-seek inside and around
the latrine that revolves in the summer twilight;
the sunset's beauty, its look of reproach;

all that weighs upon one, entwines one, wounds one;
an electric sign's tears on the opposite bank;
through the mist the stream of its emeralds running;
all the things that already I cannot express.

In a moment we'll pass across the world's threshold
into a region—name it as you please:
wilderness, death, disavowal of language,
or maybe simpler: the silence of love;

the silence of a distant cartway, its furrow,
beneath the foam of flowers concealed;
my silent country (the love that is hopeless);
the silent sheet lightning, the silent seed.

Signed: Vasiliy Shishkov

*The Russian original appeared in October or November,
1939, in the* Russkiya Zapiski, *if I remember correctly, and*

was acclaimed by Adamovich in his review of that issue with quite exceptional enthusiasm. ("At last a great poet has been born in our midst," etc.—I quote from memory, but I believe a bibliographer is in the process of tracking down this item.) I could not resist elaborating the fun and, shortly after the eulogy appeared, I published in the same Posl. Nov. *(December 1939? Here again the precise date eludes me) my prose piece "Vasiliy Shishkov" (collected in* Vesna v Fialte, *New York, 1956) which could be regarded, according to the émigré reader's degree of acumen, either as an actual occurrence involving a real person called Shishkov, or as a tongue-in-cheek story about the strange case of one poet dissolving in another. Adamovich refused at first to believe eager friends and foes who drew his attention to my having invented Shishkov; finally, he gave in and explained in his next essay that I "was a sufficiently skillful parodist to mimic genius." I fervently wish all critics to be as generous as he. I met him, briefly, only twice; but many old literati have spoken a lot, on the occasion of his recent death, about his kindliness and penetrativeness. He had really only two passions in life: Russian poetry and French sailors.*

THE LITTLE I remember about him is centered within the confines of last spring: the spring of 1939. I had been to some "Evening of Russian Emigré Literature"—one of those boring affairs so current in Paris since the early twenties. As I was quickly descending the stairs (an intermission having given me the opportunity to escape), I seemed to hear the gallop of eager pursuit behind me; I looked back, and this is when I saw him for the first time. From a couple of steps above me where he had come to a stop, he said: "My name is Vasiliy Shishkov. I am a poet."

Then he came down to my level—a solidly built young man of an eminently Russian type, thicklipped and gray-eyed, with a deep voice and a capacious, comfortable handshake.

"I want to consult you about something," he continued. "A meeting between us would be desirable."

I am a person not spoiled by such desires. My assent all but brimmed with tender emotion. We decided he would see me next day at my shabby hotel (grandly named Royal Versailles). Very punctually I came down into the simulacrum of a lounge which was comparatively quiet at that hour, if one discounted the convulsive exertions of the lift, and the conversation conducted in their accustomed corner by four German refugees who were discussing certain intricacies of the *carte d'identité* system. One of them apparently thought that his plight was not as bad as that of the others, and the others argued that it was exactly the same. Then a fifth appeared and greeted his compatriots for some reason in French: facetiousness? Swank? The lure of a new language? He had just bought a hat; they all started trying it on.

Shishkov entered. With a serious expression on his face and something equally serious in the thrust of his shoulder, he overcame the rusty reluctance of the revolving door and barely had time to look around before he saw me. Here I noted with pleasure that he eschewed the conventional grin which I fear so greatly—and to which I myself am prone. I had some difficulty in drawing together two over-stuffed armchairs—and again I found most pleasing that instead of sketching a mechanical gesture of cooperation, he remained standing at ease, his hands in the pockets of his ancient trench coat, waiting for me to arrange our seats. As soon as we had settled down, he produced a tawny notebook.

"First of all," said Shishkov, fixing me with nice, furry eyes, "a person must produce his credentials—am I right? At the police station I would have shown my identity card, and to you, Gospodin Nabokov, I must show this —a cahier of verse."

I leafed through it. The firm handwriting, slightly inclined to the left, emanated health and talent. Alas, once my glance went zigzagging down the lines, I felt a pang of disappointment. The poetry was dreadful—flat, flashy, ominously pretentious. Its utter mediocrity was stressed by the fraudulent chic of alliterations and the meretricious richness of illiterate rhymes. Sufficent to say that such pairs were formed as, for example, *teatr–gladiator*, *mustang–tank*, *Madonna–belladonna*. As to the themes, they were best left alone: the author sang with unvarying gusto anything that his lyre came across. Reading his poems one after the other was torture for a nervous person, but since my conscientiousness happened to be reinforced by the author's watching closely over me and controlling both the direction of my gaze and the action of my fingers, I found myself obliged to stop for a few moments at every consecutive page.

"Well, what's the verdict?" he asked when I had finished: "Not too awful?"

I considered him. His somewhat glossy face with enlarged pores expressed no ominous premonition whatever. I replied that his poetry was hopelessly bad. Shishkov clicked his tongue, thrust the notebook back into the pocket of his trench coat, and said:

"Those credentials are not mine. I mean, I did write that stuff myself, and yet it is all forged. The entire lot of thirty poems was composed this morning, and to tell the truth, I found rather nasty the task of parodying the product of metromania. In return, I now have learned that you are merciless—which means that you can be trusted. Here is my real passport." (Shishkov handed me another, much more tattered, notebook.) "Read just one poem at random, it will be enough for both you and me. By the way, to avoid any misapprehension, let me warn you that I do not care for your novels, they irritate me as would a harsh light or the loud conversation of strangers when one longs not to talk, but to think. Yet, at the same time, in a purely physiological way—if I may put it like that—you possess some secret of writing, the secret of certain basic colors, something exceptionally rare and important, which, alas, you apply to little purpose, within the narrow limits of your general abilities—driving about, so to speak, all over the place in a powerful racing car for which you have absolutely no use, but which keeps you thinking where could one thunder off next. However, as you possess that secret, people must reckon with you—and this is why I should like to enlist your support in a certain matter; but first take, please, a look at my poems."

(I must admit that the unexpected and uncalled-for lecture on the character of my literary work struck me as considerably more impudent than the harmless bit of deception my visitor had devised. I write for the sake of concrete pleasure and publish my writings for the sake of much less concrete money, and though the latter point should imply, in one way or another, the existence of a consumer, it always seems to me that the farther my published books, in the course of their natural evolution, retreat from their self-contained source, the more abstract and insignificant become the fortuitous events of their career. As to the so-called Readers' Judgment, I feel, at that trial, not as the defendant, but, at best, as a distant relative of one of the least important witnesses. In other words a reviewer's praise seems to me an odd kind of *sans-gêne*, and his abuse, a vain lunge at a specter. At the moment, I was trying to decide whether Shishkov tumbled his candid opinion into the lap of every proud writer he met or whether it was only with me that he was so blunt because he believed I deserved it. I concluded that just as the doggerel trick had been a result of his somewhat childish but genuine thirst for truth, so the voicing of his views about me was prompted by the urge of widening to the utmost the frame of mutual frankness.)

I vaguely feared that the genuine product might reveal traces of the defects monstrously exaggerated in the parody, but my fears proved unfounded. The poems were very good—I hope to discuss them some other time in much greater detail. Recently, I was instrumental in getting one published in an émigré magazine, and lovers of poetry noticed its originality.* To the poet that was so strangely gourmand in regard to another's opinion, I incontinently expressed mine, adding, as a corrective, that the poem in question contained some tiny fluctuations of style such as, for instance, the not quite idiomatic *v soldatskih mundirah*; here *mundir* (uniform) should rather be *forma* when referring as it did to the lower ranks. The line, however was much too good to be tampered with.

"You know what," said Shishkov, "since you agree with me that my poems are not trifles, let me leave that book in your keeping. One never knows what may happen; strange, very strange thoughts occur to me, and—— Well, anyway, everything now turns out admirably. You see, my object in visiting you was to ask you to take part in a new magazine I am planning to launch. Saturday there will be a gathering at my place and everything must be decided. Naturally, I cherish no illusions concerning your capacity for being carried away by the problems of the modern world, but I think the idea of that journal might interest you from a stylistic point of view. So, please, come. Incidentally, we expect" (Shishkov named an extremely famous Russian writer) "and some other prominent people. You have to understand—I have reached a certain limit, I abso-

* See prefatory note, p. 206.

lutely must take the strain off, or else I'll go mad. I'll be thirty soon; last year I came here, to Paris, after an utterly sterile adolescence in the Balkans and then in Austria. I am working here as a bookbinder but I have been a typesetter and even a librarian—in short I have always rubbed against books. Yet, I repeat, my life has been sterile, and, of late, I'm bursting with the urge to do something—a most agonizing sensation—for you must see yourself, from another angle, perhaps, but still you *must* see, how much suffering, imbecility, and filth surrounds us; yet people of my generation notice nothing, do nothing, though action is simply as necessary as, say, breath or bread. And mind you, I speak not of big, burning questions that have bored everybody to death, but of a trillion trivia which people do not perceive, although they, those trifles, are the embryos of most obvious monsters. Just the other day, for example, a mother, having lost patience, drowned her two-year-old daughter in the bathtub and then took a bath in the same water, because it was hot, and hot water should not be squandered. Good God, how far this is from the old peasant woman, in one of Turgenev's turgid little tales, who had just lost her son and shocked the fine lady who visited her in her izba by calmly finishing a bowl of cabbage soup 'because it had been salted'! I shan't mind in the least if you regard as absurd the fact that the tremendous number of similar trifles, every day, everywhere, of various degree of importance and of different shape—tailed germs, punctiform, cubic— can trouble a man so badly that he suffocates and loses his appetite—but, maybe, you will come all the same."

I have combined here our conversation at the Royal Versailles with excerpts from a diffuse letter that Shishkov sent me next day by way of corroboration. On the following Saturday I was a little late for the meeting, so that when I entered his *chambre garnie* which was as modest as it was tidy, all were assembled, excepting the famous writer. Among those present, I knew by sight the editor of a defunct publication; the others—an ample female (a translatress, I believe, or perhaps a theosophist) with a gloomy little husband resembling a black breloque; her old mother; two seedy gentlemen in the kind of ill-fitting suits that the émigré cartoonist Mad gives to his characters; and an energetic-looking blond fellow, our host's chum—were unknown to me. Upon observing that Shishkov kept cocking an anxious ear—observing, too, how resolutely and joyfully he clapped the table and rose, before realizing that the doorbell he had heard pertained to another apartment—I ardently hoped for the celebrity's arrival, but the old boy never turned up.

"Ladies and gentlemen," said Shishkov and began to develop, quite eloquently and engagingly, his plans for a monthly, which would be entitled "A Survey of Pain and Vulgarity" and would mainly consist of a collection of relevant newspaper items for the month, with the stipulation that they be arranged not chronologically but in an "ascending" and "artistically unobtrusive" sequence. The one-time editor quoted certain figures and declared he was perfectly sure that a Russian émigré review of that sort would never sell. The husband of the ample literary lady removed his pince-nez and, while massaging the bridge of his nose, said with horrible haws and hems that if the intention was to fight human misery, it might be much more practical to distribute among the poor the sum of money needed for the review; and since it was from him one expected that money, a chill came over the listeners. After that, the host's friend repeated—in brisker but baser terms —what Shishkov had already stated. My opinion was also asked. The expression on Shishkov's face was so tragic that I did my best to champion his project. We dispersed rather early. As he was accompanying us to the landing, Shishkov slipped and, a little longer than was required to encourage the general laughter, remained sitting on the floor with a cheerful smile and impossible eyes.

A fortnight later he again came to see me, and again the four German refugees were discussing passport problems, and presently a fifth entered and cheerfully said: "*Bonjour, Monsieur Weiss, bonjour, Monsieur Meyer.*" To my questions, Shishkov replied, rather absently and as it were reluctantly, that the idea of his journal had been found unrealizable, and that he had stopped thinking about it.

"Here's what I wanted to tell you," he began after an uneasy silence: "I have been trying and trying to come to a decision and now I think I have hit upon something, more or less. *Why* I am in this terrible state would hardly interest you; I explained what I could in my letter but that concerned mainly the business in hand, the magazine. The question is more extensive, the question is more hopeless. I have been trying to decide what to do—how to stop things, how to get out. Beat it to Africa, to the colonies? But it is hardly worth starting the Herculean task of obtaining the necessary papers only to find myself pondering in the midst of date palms and scorpions the same things I ponder under the Paris rain. Try making my way back to Russia? No, the frying pan is enough. Retire to a monastery? But religion is boring and alien to me and relates no more than a chimera to what is to me the reality of the spirit. Commit suicide? But capital punishment is something I find too repulsive to be able to act as my own executioner, and, furthermore, I dread certain consequences undreamt of in Hamlet's philosophy. Thus there remains but one issue: to disappear, to dissolve."

He inquired further whether his manuscript was safe, and shortly afterwards left, broad-shouldered yet a little stooped, trench-coated, hatless, the back of his neck needing a haircut—an extraordinarily attractive, pure, melancholy human being, to whom I did not know what to say, what assistance to render.

In late May I left for another part of France and upon returning to Paris at the end of August happened to run into Shishkov's friend. He told me a bizarre story: some time after my departure, "Vasya" had vanished, abandoning his meager belongings. The police could discover nothing—beyond the fact that *le sieur Chichkoff* had long since allowed his *karta*, as the Russians call it, to run out.

That is all. With the kind of incident that opens a mystery story my narrative closes. I got from his friend, or rather chance acquaintance, bits of scant information about Shishkov's life and these I jotted down—they may prove useful some day. But where the deuce did he go? And, generally speaking, what did he have in mind when he said he intended "to disappear, to dissolve"? Cannot it actually be that in a wildly literal sense, unacceptable to one's reason, he meant disappearing in his art, dissolving in his verse, thus leaving of himself, of his nebulous person, nothing but verse? One wonders if he did not overestimate

The transparence and soundness
Of such an unusual coffin.

THE VANE SISTERS

Written in Ithaca, New York, in February 1951. First published in The Hudson Review, *New York, Winter 1959, and in* Encounter, *London, March 1959. Reprinted in the collection* Nabokov's Quartet, Phaedra Publishers, *New York, 1966.*

In this story the narrator is supposed to be unaware that his last paragraph has been used acrostically by two dead girls to assert their mysterious participation in the story. This particular trick can be tried only once in a thousand years of fiction. Whether it has come off is another question.

1

I MIGHT never have heard of Cynthia's death, had I not run, that night, into D., whom I had also lost track of for the last four years or so; and I might never have run into D. had I not got involved in a series of trivial investigations.

The day, a compunctious Sunday after a week of blizzards, had been part jewel, part mud. In the midst of my usual afternoon stroll through the small hilly town attached to the girls' college where I taught French literature, I had stopped to watch a family of brilliant icicles drip-dripping from the eaves of a frame house. So clear-cut were their pointed shadows on the white boards behind them that I was sure the shadows of the falling drops should be visible too. But they were not. The roof jutted too far out, perhaps, or the angle of vision was faulty, or, again, I did not chance to be watching the right icicle when the right drop fell. There was a rhythm, an alternation in the dripping that I found as teasing as a coin trick. It led me to inspect the corners of several house blocks, and this brought me to Kelly Road, and right to the house where D. used to live when he was instructor here. And as I looked up at the eaves of the adjacent garage with its full display of transparent stalactites backed by their blue silhouettes, I was rewarded at last, upon choosing one, by the sight of what might be described as the dot of an exclamation mark leaving its ordinary position to glide down very fast—a jot faster than the thaw-drop it raced. This twinned twinkle was delightful but not completely satisfying; or rather it only sharpened my appetite for other tidbits of light and shade, and I walked on in a state of raw awareness that seemed to transform the whole of my being into one big eyeball rolling in the world's socket.

Through peacocked lashes I saw the dazzling diamond reflection of the low sun on the round back of a parked automobile. To all kinds of things a vivid pictorial sense had been restored by the sponge of the thaw. Water in overlapping festoons flowed down one sloping street and turned gracefully into another. With ever so slight a note of meretricious appeal, narrow passages between buildings revealed treasures of brick and purple. I remarked for the first time the humble fluting—last echoes of grooves on the shafts of columns—ornamenting a garbage can, and I also saw the rippling upon its lid—circles diverging from a fantastically ancient center. Erect, dark-headed shapes of dead snow (left by the blades of a bulldozer last Friday) were lined up like rudimentary penguins along the curbs, above the brilliant vibration of live gutters.

I walked up, and I walked down, and I walked straight into a delicately dying sky, and finally the sequence of observed and observant things brought me, at my usual eating time, to a street so distant from my usual eating place that I decided to try a restaurant which stood on the fringe of the town. Night had fallen without sound or ceremony when I came out again. The lean ghost, the elongated umbra cast by a parking meter upon some damp snow, had a strange ruddy tinge; this I made out to be due to the tawny red light of the restaurant sign above the sidewalk; and it was then—as I loitered there, wondering rather wearily if in the course of my return tramp I might be lucky enough to find the same in neon blue—it was then that a car crunched to a standstill near me and D. got out of it with an exclamation of feigned pleasure.

He was passing, on his way from Albany to Boston, through the town he had dwelt in before, and more than once in my life have I felt that stab of vicarious emotion followed by a rush of personal irritation against travelers who seem to feel nothing at all upon revisiting spots that ought to harass them at every step with wailing and writhing memories. He ushered me back into the bar that I had just left, and after the usual exchange of buoyant platitudes came the inevitable vacuum which he filled with the random words: "Say, I never thought there was anything wrong with Cynthia Vane's heart. My lawyer tells me she died last week."

2

He was still young, still brash, still shifty, still married to the gentle, exquisitely pretty woman who had never learned or suspected anything about his disastrous affair with Cynthia's hysterical young sister, who in her turn had known nothing of the interview I had had with Cynthia when she suddenly summoned me to Boston to make me swear I would talk to D. and get him "kicked out" if he did not stop seeing Sybil at once—or did not divorce his wife (whom incidentally she visualized through the prism of Sybil's wild talk as a termagant and a fright). I had cornered him immediately. He had said there was nothing to worry about—had made up his mind, anyway, to give up his college job and move with his wife to Albany, where he would work in his father's firm; and the whole matter, which had threatened to become one of those hopelessly entangled situations that drag on for years, with peripheral sets of well-meaning friends endlessly discussing it in universal secrecy—and even founding, among themselves, new intimacies upon its alien woes—came to an abrupt end.

I remember sitting next day at my raised desk in the large classroom where a mid-year examination in French Lit. was being held on the eve of Sybil's suicide. She came in on high heels, with a suitcase, dumped it in a corner where several other bags were stacked, with a single shrug slipped her fur coat off her thin shoulders, folded it on her bag, and with two or three other girls stopped before my desk to ask when would I mail them their grades. It would take me a week, beginning from tomorrow, I said, to read the stuff. I also remember wondering whether D. had already informed her of his decision—and I felt acutely unhappy about my dutiful little student as during one hundred and fifty minutes my gaze kept reverting to her, so childishly slight in close-fitting gray, and kept observing that carefully waved dark hair, that small, small-flowered hat with a little hyaline veil as worn that season and under it her small face broken into a cubist pattern by scars due to a skin disease, pathetically masked by a sunlamp tan that hardened her features, whose charm was further impaired by her having painted everything that could be painted, so that the pale gums of her teeth between cherry-red chapped lips and the diluted blue ink of her eyes under darkened lids were the only visible openings into her beauty.

Next day, having arranged the ugly copybooks alphabetically, I plunged into their chaos of scripts and came prematurely to Valevsky and Vane, whose books I had somehow misplaced. The first was dressed up for the occasion in a semblance of legibility, but Sybil's work displayed her usual combination of several demon hands. She had begun in very pale, very hard pencil which had conspicuously embossed the blank verso, but had produced little of permanent value on the upper side of the page. Happily the tip soon broke, and Sybil continued in another, darker lead, gradually lapsing into the blurred thickness of what looked almost like charcoal, to which, by sucking the blunt point, she had contributed some traces of lipstick. Her work, although even poorer than I had expected, bore all the signs of a kind of desperate conscientiousness, with underscores, transposes, unnecessary footnotes, as if she were intent upon rounding up things in the most respectable manner possible. Then she had borrowed Mary Valevsky's fountain pen and added: "*Cette examain est finie ainsi que ma vie. Adieu, jeunes filles!* Please, *Monsieur le Professeur,* contact *ma soeur* and tell her that Death was not better than D minus, but definitely better than Life minus D."

I lost no time in ringing up Cynthia, who told me it was all over—had been all over since eight in the morning—and asked me to bring her the note, and when I did, beamed through her tears with proud admiration for the whimsical use ("Just like her!") Sybil had made of an examination in French literature. In no time she "fixed" two highballs, while never parting with Sybil's notebook—by now splashed with soda water and tears—and went on studying the death message, whereupon I was impelled to point out to her the grammatical mistakes in it and to explain the way "girl" is translated in American colleges lest students innocently bandy around the French equivalent of "wench," or worse. These rather tasteless trivialities pleased Cynthia hugely as she rose, with gasps, above the heaving surface of her grief. And then, holding that limp notebook as if it were a kind of passport to a casual Elysium (where pencil points do not snap and a dreamy young beauty with an impeccable complexion winds a lock of her hair on a dreamy forefinger, as she meditates over some celestial test), Cynthia led me upstairs to a chilly little bedroom, just to show me, as if I were the police or a sympathetic Irish neighbor, two empty pill bottles and the tumbled bed from which a tender, inessential body, that D. must have known down to its last velvet detail, had been already removed.

3

It was four or five months after her sister's death that I began seeing Cynthia fairly often. By the time I had come to New York for some vacational research in the Public Library she had also moved to that city, where for some odd reason (in vague connection, I presume, with artistic motives) she had taken what people, immune to gooseflesh, term a "cold water" flat, down in the scale of the city's transverse streets. What attracted me was neither her ways, which I thought repulsively vivacious, nor her looks, which other men thought striking. She had widespaced eyes very much like her sister's, of a frank, frightened blue with dark points in a radial arrangement. The interval between her thick black eyebrows was always shiny, and shiny too were the fleshy volutes of her nostrils. The coarse texture of her epiderm looked almost masculine, and, in the stark lamplight of her studio, you could see the pores of her thirty-two-year-old face fairly gaping at you like something in an aquarium. She used cosmetics with as much zest as her little sister had, but with an additional slovenliness that would result in her big front teeth getting some of the rouge. She was handsomely dark, wore a not too tasteless mixture of fairly smart heterogeneous things, and had a so-called good figure; but all of her was curiously frowzy, after a way I obscurely associated with left-wing enthusiasms in politics and "advanced" banalities in art, although, actually, she cared for neither. Her coily hair-do, on a part-and-bun basis, might have looked feral and bizarre had it not been thoroughly domesticated by its own soft unkemptness at the vulnerable nape. Her fingernails were gaudily painted, but badly bitten and not clean. Her lovers were a silent young photographer with a sudden laugh and two older men, brothers, who owned a small printing establishment across the street. I wondered at their tastes whenever I glimpsed, with a secret shudder, the higgledy-piggledy striation of black hairs that showed all along her pale shins through the nylon of her stockings with the scientific distinctness of a preparation flattened under glass; or when I felt, at her every movement, the dullish, stalish, not particularly conspicuous but all-pervading and depressing emanation that her seldom bathed flesh spread from under weary perfumes and creams.

Her father had gambled away the greater part of a comfortable fortune, and her mother's first husband had been of Slav origin, but otherwise Cynthia Vane belonged to a good, respectable family. For aught we know, it may have gone back to kings and soothsayers in the mists of ultimate islands. Transferred to a newer world, to a landscape of doomed, splendid deciduous trees, her ancestry presented, in one of its first phases, a white churchful of farmers against a black thunderhead, and then an imposing array of townsmen engaged in mercantile pursuits, as well as a number of learned men, such as Dr. Jonathan Vane, the gaunt bore (1780–1839), who perished in the conflagration of the steamer *Lexington* to become later an habitué of Cynthia's tilting table. I have always wished to stand genealogy on its head, and here I have an opportunity to do so, for it is the last scion, Cynthia, and Cynthia alone, who will remain of any importance in the Vane dynasty. I am alluding of course to her artistic gift, to her delightful, gay, but not very popular paintings, which the friends of her friends bought at long intervals—and I dearly should like to know where they went after her death, those honest and poetical pictures that illumined her living room—the wonderfully detailed images of metallic things, and my favorite "Seen Through a Windshield"—a windshield partly covered with rime, with a brilliant trickle (from an imaginary car roof) across its transparent part and, through it all, the sapphire flame of the sky and a green and white fir tree.

4

Cynthia had a feeling that her dead sister was not altogether pleased with her—had discovered by now that she and I had conspired to break her romance; and so, in order to disarm her shade, Cynthia reverted to a rather primitive type of sacrificial offering (tinged, however, with something of Sybil's humor), and began to send to D.'s business address, at deliberately unfixed dates, such trifles as snapshots of Sybil's tomb in a poor light; cuttings of her own hair which was indistinguishable from Sybil's; a New England sectional map with an inked-in cross, midway between two chaste towns, to mark the spot where D. and Sybil had stopped on October the twenty-third, in broad daylight, at a lenient motel, in a pink and brown forest; and, twice, a stuffed skunk.

Being as a conversationalist more voluble than explicit, she never could describe in full the theory of intervenient auras that she had somehow evolved. Fundamentally there was nothing particularly new about her private creed since it presupposed a fairly conventional hereafter, a silent solarium of immortal souls (spliced with mortal antecedents) whose main recreation consisted of periodical hoverings over the dear quick. The interesting point was a curious practical twist that Cynthia gave to her tame metaphysics. She was sure that her existence was influenced by all sorts of dead friends each of whom took turns in directing her fate much as if she were a stray kitten which a schoolgirl in passing gathers up, and presses to her cheek, and carefully puts down again, near some suburban hedge—to be stroked presently by another transient hand or carried off to a world of doors by some hospitable lady.

For a few hours, or for several days in a row, and sometimes recurrently, in an irregular series, for months or years, anything that happened to Cynthia, after a given person had died, would be, she said, in the manner and mood of that person. The event might be extraordinary, changing the course of one's life; or it might be a string of minute incidents just sufficiently clear to stand out in relief against one's usual day and then shading off into still vaguer trivia as the aura gradually faded. The influence might be good or bad; the main thing was that its source could be identified. It was like walking through a person's soul, she said. I tried to argue that she might not always be able to determine the exact source since not everybody has a recognizable soul; that there are anonymous letters and Christmas presents which anybody might send; that, in fact, what Cynthia called "a usual day" might be itself a weak solution of mixed auras or simply the routine shift of a humdrum guardian angel. And what about God? Did or did not people who would resent any omnipotent dictator on earth look forward to one in heaven? And wars? What a dreadful idea—dead soldiers still fighting with living ones, or phantom armies trying to get at each other through the lives of crippled old men.

But Cynthia was above generalities as she was beyond logic. "Ah, that's Paul," she would say when the soup spitefully boiled over, or: "I guess good Betty Brown is dead" when she won a beautiful and very welcome vacuum cleaner in a charity lottery. And, with Jamesian meanderings that exasperated my French mind, she would go back to a time when Betty and Paul had not yet departed, and tell me of the showers of well-meant, but odd and quite unacceptable, bounties—beginning with an old purse that contained a check for three dollars which she picked up in the street and, of course, returned (to the aforesaid Betty Brown—this is where she first comes in—a decrepit colored woman hardly able to walk), and ending with an insulting proposal from an old beau of hers (this is where Paul comes in) to paint "straight" pictures of his house and family for a reasonable remuneration—all of which followed upon the demise of a certain Mrs. Page, a kindly but petty old party who had pestered her with bits of matter-of-fact advice since Cynthia had been a child.

Sybil's personality, she said, had a rainbow edge as if a little out of focus. She said that had I known Sybil better I would have at once understood how Sybil-like was the aura of minor events which, in spells, had suffused her, Cynthia's, existence after Sybil's suicide. Ever since they had lost their mother they had intended to give up their Boston home and move to New York, where Cynthia's paintings, they thought, would have a chance to be more widely admired; but the old home had clung to them with all its plush tentacles. Dead Sybil, however, had proceeded to separate the house from its view—a thing that affects fatally the sense of home. Right across the narrow street a building project had come into loud, ugly, scaffolded life. A pair of familiar poplars died that spring, turning to blond skeletons. Workmen came and broke up the warm-colored lovely old sidewalk that had a special violet sheen on wet April days and had echoed so memorably to the morning footsteps of museum-bound Mr. Lever, who upon retiring from business at sixty had devoted a full quarter of a century exclusively to the study of snails.

Speaking of old men, one should add that sometimes these posthumous auspices and interventions were in the nature of parody. Cynthia had been on friendly terms with an eccentric librarian called Porlock who in the last years of his dusty life had been engaged in examining old books for miraculous misprints such as the substitution of "l" for the second "h" in the word "hither." Contrary to Cynthia, he cared nothing for the thrill of obscure predictions; all he sought was the freak itself, the chance that mimics choice, the flaw that looks like a flower; and Cynthia, a much more perverse amateur of misshapen or illicitly connected words, puns, logogriphs, and so on, had helped the poor crank to pursue a quest that in the light of the example she cited struck me as statistically insane. Anyway, she said, on the third day after his death she was reading a magazine and had just come across a quotation from an imperishable poem (that she, with other gullible readers, believed to have been really composed in a dream) when it dawned upon her that "Alph" was a prophetic sequence of the initial letters of Anna Livia Plurabelle (another sacred river running through, or rather around, yet another fake dream), while the additional "h" modestly stood, as a private signpost, for the word that had so hypnotized Mr. Porlock. And I wish I could recollect that novel or short story (by some contemporary writer, I believe) in which, unknown to its author, the first letters of the words in its last paragraph formed, as deciphered by Cynthia, a message from his dead mother.

5

I am sorry to say that not content with these ingenious fancies Cynthia showed a ridiculous fondness for spiritualism. I refused to accompany her to sittings in which paid mediums took part: I knew too much about that from other sources. I did consent, however, to attend little farces rigged up by Cynthia and her two poker-faced gentlemen-friends of the printing shop. They were podgy, polite, and rather eerie old fellows, but I satisfied myself that they possessed considerable wit and culture. We sat down at a light little table, and crackling tremors started almost as soon as we laid our fingertips upon it. I was treated to an assortment of ghosts that rapped out their reports most readily though refusing to elucidate anything that I did not quite catch. Oscar Wilde came in and in rapid garbled French, with the usual anglicisms, obscurely accused Cynthia's dead parents of what appeared in my jottings as "*plagiatisme.*" A brisk spirit contributed the unsolicited information that he, John Moore, and his brother Bill had been coal miners in Colorado and had perished in an avalanche at "Crested Beauty" in January 1883. Frederic Myers, an old hand at the game, hammered out a piece of verse (oddly resembling Cynthia's own fugitive productions) which in part reads in my notes:

> *What is this—a conjurer's rabbit,*
> *Or a flawy but genuine gleam—*
> *Which can check the perilous habit*
> *And dispel the dolorous dream?*

Finally, with a great crash and all kinds of shudderings and jiglike movements on the part of the table, Leo Tolstoy visited our little group and, when asked to identify himself by specific traits of terrene habitation, launched upon a complex description of what seemed to be some Russian type of architectural woodwork ("figures on boards—man, horse, cock, man, horse, cock"), all of which was difficult to take down, hard to understand, and impossible to verify.

I attended two or three other sittings which were even sillier but I must confess that I preferred the childish entertainment they afforded and the cider we drank (Podgy and Pudgy were teetotalers) to Cynthia's awful house parties.

She gave them at the Wheelers' nice flat next door—the sort of arrangement dear to her centrifugal nature, but then, of course, her own living room always looked like a dirty old palette. Following a barbaric, unhygienic, and adulterous custom, the guests' coats, still warm on the inside, were carried by quiet, baldish Bob Wheeler into the sanctity of a tidy bedroom and heaped on the conjugal bed. It was also he who poured out the drinks, which were passed around by the young photographer while Cynthia and Mrs. Wheeler took care of the canapés.

A late arrival had the impression of lots of loud people unnecessarily grouped within a smoke-blue space between two mirrors gorged with reflections. Because, I suppose, Cynthia wished to be the youngest in the room, the women she used to invite, married or single, were, at the best, in their precarious forties; some of them would bring from their homes, in dark taxis, intact vestiges of good looks, which, however, they lost as the party progressed. It has always amazed me the ability sociable weekend revelers have of finding almost at once, by a purely empiric but very precise method, a common denominator of drunkenness, to which everybody loyally sticks before descending, all together, to the next level. The rich friendliness of the matrons was marked by tomboyish overtones, while the fixed inward look of amiably tight men was like a sacrilegious parody of pregnancy. Although some of the guests were connected in one way or another with the arts, there was no inspired talk, no wreathed, elbow-propped heads, and of course no flute girls. From some vantage point where she had been sitting in a stranded mermaid pose on the pale carpet with one or two younger fellows, Cynthia, her face varnished with a film of beaming sweat, would creep up on her knees, a proffered plate of nuts in one hand, and crisply tap with the other the athletic leg of Cochran or Corcoran, an art dealer, ensconced, on a pearl-gray sofa, between two flushed, happily disintegrating ladies.

At a further stage there would come spurts of more riotous gaiety. Corcoran or Coransky would grab Cynthia or some other wandering woman by the shoulder and lead her into a corner to confront her with a grinning embroglio of private jokes and rumors, whereupon, with a laugh and a toss of her head, she would break away. And still later there would be flurries of intersexual chumminess, jocular reconciliations, a bare fleshy arm flung around another woman's husband (he standing very upright in the midst of a swaying room), or a sudden rush of flirtatious anger, of clumsy pursuit—and the quiet half smile of Bob Wheeler picking up glasses that grew like mushrooms in the shade of chairs.

After one last party of that sort, I wrote Cynthia a perfectly harmless and, on the whole, well-meant note, in which I poked a little Latin fun at some of her guests. I also apologized for not having touched her whiskey, saying that as a Frenchman I preferred the grape to the grain. A few days later I met her on the steps of the Public Library, in the broken sun, under a weak cloudburst, opening her amber umbrella, struggling with a couple of armpitted books (of which I relieved her for a moment), *Footfalls on the Boundary of Another World,* by Robert Dale Owen, and something on "Spiritualism and Christianity"; when, suddenly, with no provocation on my part, she blazed out at me with vulgar vehemence, using poisonous words, saying—through pear-shaped drops of sparse rain—that I was a prig and a snob; that I only saw the gestures and disguises of people; that Corcoran had rescued from drowning, in two different oceans, two men—by an irrelevant coincidence both called Corcoran; that romping and screeching Joan Winter had a little girl doomed to grow completely blind in a few months; and that the woman in green with the freckled chest whom I had snubbed in some way or other had written a national best seller in 1932. Strange Cynthia! I had been told she could be thunderously rude to people whom she liked and respected; one had, however, to draw the line somewhere and since I had by then sufficiently studied her interesting auras and other odds and ids, I decided to stop seeing her altogether.

6

The night D. informed me of Cynthia's death I returned after eleven to the two-story house I shared, in horizontal section, with an emeritus professor's widow. Upon reaching the porch I looked with the apprehension of solitude at the two kinds of darkness in the two rows of windows: the darkness of absence and the darkness of sleep.

I could do something about the first but could not duplicate the second. My bed gave me no sense of safety; its springs only made my nerves bounce. I plunged into Shakespeare's sonnets—and found myself idiotically checking the first letters of the lines to see what sacramental words they might form. I got FATE (LXX), ATOM (CXX) and, twice, TAFT (LXXXVIII, CXXXI). Every now and then I would glance around to see how the objects in my room were behaving. It was strange to think that if bombs began to fall I would feel little more than a gambler's excitement (and a great deal of earthy relief) whereas my heart would burst if a certain suspiciously tense-looking little bottle on yonder shelf moved a fraction of an inch to one side. The silence, too, was suspiciously compact as if deliberately forming a black backdrop for the nerve flash caused by any small sound of unknown origin. All traffic was dead. In vain did I pray for the groan of a truck up Perkins Street. The woman above who used to drive me crazy by the booming thuds occasioned by what seemed monstrous feet of stone (actually, in diurnal life, she was a small dumpy creature resembling a mummified guinea pig) would have earned my blessings had she now trudged to her bathroom. I put out my light and cleared my throat several times so as to be responsible for at least *that* sound. I thumbed a mental ride with a very remote automobile but it dropped me before I had a chance to doze off. Presently a crackle (due, I hoped, to a discarded and crushed sheet of paper opening like a mean, stubborn night flower) —started and stopped in the wastepaper basket, and my bed table responded with a little click. It would have been just like Cynthia to put on right then a cheap poltergeist show.

I decided to fight Cynthia. I reviewed in thought the modern era of raps and apparitions, beginning with the knockings of 1848, at the hamlet of Hydesville, New York, and ending with grotesque phenomena at Cambridge, Massachusetts; I evoked the ankle bones and other anatomical castanets of the Fox sisters (as described by the sages of the University of Buffalo); the mysteriously uniform type of delicate adolescent in bleak Epworth or Tedworth, radiating the same disturbances as in old Peru; solemn Victorian orgies with roses falling and accordions floating to the strains of sacred music; professional impostors regurgitating moist cheesecloth; Mr. Duncan, a lady medium's dignified husband, who, when asked if he would submit to a search, excused himself on the ground of soiled underwear; old Alfred Russel Wallace, the naive naturalist, refusing to believe that the white form with bare feet and unperforated earlobes before him, at a private pandemonium in Boston, could be prim Miss Cook whom he had just seen asleep, in her curtained corner, all dressed in black, wearing laced-up boots and earrings; two other investigators, small, puny, but reasonably intelligent and active men, closely clinging with arms and legs about Eusapia, a large, plump elderly female reeking of garlic, who still managed to fool them; and the skeptical and embarrassed magician, instructed by charming young Margery's "control" not to get lost in the bathrobe's lining but to follow up the left stocking until he reached the bare thigh—upon the warm skin of which he felt a "teleplastic" mass that appeared to the touch uncommonly like cold, uncooked liver.

7

I was appealing to flesh, and the corruption of flesh, to refute and defeat the possible persistence of discarnate life. Alas, these conjurations only enhanced my fear of Cynthia's phantom. Atavistic peace came with dawn, and when I slipped into sleep the sun through the tawny window shades penetrated a dream that somehow was full of Cynthia.

This was disappointing. Secure in the fortress of daylight, I said to myself that I had expected more. She, a painter of glass-bright minutiae—and now so vague! I lay in bed, thinking my dream over and listening to the sparrows outside: Who knows, if recorded and then run backward, those bird sounds might not become human speech, voiced words, just as the latter become a twitter when reversed? I set myself to reread my dream—backward, diagonally, up, down—trying hard to unravel something Cynthia-like in it, something strange and suggestive that must be there.

I could isolate, consciously, little. Everything seemed blurred, yellow-clouded, yielding nothing tangible. Her inept acrostics, maudlin evasions, theopathies—every recollection formed ripples of mysterious meaning. Everything seemed yellowly blurred, illusive, lost.